MISADVENTURES

OF A

CURVY GIRL

BY
SIERRA SIMONE

MISADVENTURES OF A CURVY GIRL

BY
SIERRA SIMONE

WATERHOUSE PRESS

For Julie

CHAPTER ONE

IRELAND

The car was my first mistake.

I can admit that now, sitting here in the mud, my windshield almost too splattered with the stuff to make out the herd of cows chewing curiously at me on the other side of the fence.

With a low curse—and a glare back at the judgmental cows—I fumble for my phone, thinking I'll call someone. Anyone. A friend. A tow truck. An Uber. But when the screen lights up, I realize there's no LTE out here. There's not even 3G.

Not even 3G.

No cell service at all, actually. I throw myself back against my seat and listen to the sporadic drumming of rain on my roof. When my coworkers back at Typeset—the social media strategy firm I work for—heard I was heading out to the Flint Hills in my Prius, they laughed and teased, and a couple even offered me their trucks, but I refused. My little blue car may look like a piece of candy, but it's never let me down in the city. Not once. I didn't see any reason it would let me down just because I was a couple of hours west.

I see the reason now, I assure you. Two words: dirt roads.

I get out of the car again, pushing open my umbrella to shield me from the petulant, spitting rain while I walk around my vehicle to confirm for a final time that yes, all four tires are stuck deeply in the mud. It's rained the past three days straight—something not even worth noticing back in Kansas City except maybe to whine about how it slowed morning traffic—but out here in farm country, the rain definitely makes itself known. The roads are nothing but slicks of rough mud, and the lonely trees look huddled and limp. The long fingers of summer grass crowding up along the side of the road are battered down by the days of rain, and the wet emerald stalks peppered with yellow coneflowers and purple spiderwort look just as sodden and battered.

It *is* beautiful, though. And for a minute, I look up from my mud-bound car and just take it in—the heady abundance of green grass and wildflowers, the brooding sweep of the hills in the near distance. The line of black clouds in the west, promising rain and wind and danger. It's like something that would be printed in a calendar, and the moment I think the thought, I dive back into my car for the expensive Nikon camera in the passenger seat. And then awkwardly crawl back out, abandoning my umbrella so I can capture the moment before it vanishes—the energy, the quietly decadent riot of wildflowers, the promise of abundant prairie summer.

I take as many pictures as I can, trying to pick my way through the mud in my ballet flats, and for a brief moment, I wonder what my life would have been like if I'd taken that photography scholarship out of state instead of staying local and studying marketing all those years ago.

I wanted to see the world once. I wanted to be one of those photographers who tramps all over Patagonia and Punjab, who snaps arresting photos of little Alpine villages and intrepid Antarctic outposts. And maybe if I took enough gorgeous, stirring photos, no one would've cared the woman behind the camera wasn't gorgeous or stirring herself.

Stop it, Ireland.

This is exactly the kind of thought I am done entertaining. I turn to the car, seeing my reflection in the window just as I knew I would. I make myself look at it. Really look. Not the half-sideways glance I used to give, as if my view bounced off any mirrored surface without me actually seeing myself. No. I look, and I take in the pale twenty-four-year-old woman standing there. Ireland Mills.

She has dark hair almost to her waist because she loves having long hair.

A girl of your size really should have shorter hair.

She has wide hips and thighs in a formfitting pencil skirt, and a thin silk blouse that does nothing to hide the shape of her soft, swelling breasts.

Don't you think that's more of a "goal" outfit? For when you lose weight?

A mouth in lavender lipstick, the sweet color visible even in the faint reflection.

I wouldn't draw attention to your face if I were you. I would want to blend in.

Pursing my attention-drawing mouth, I raise the camera and take a picture of myself. It's not a coincidence all the negative thoughts in my head have my sister's voice behind them, and I'm done listening. I'm done listening to her, and I'm done listening to my ex-boyfriend, who dumped me last month when I told him I stopped my eternal diet and dropped my gym membership so I could go to dance classes instead.

"But those classes aren't designed for people to lose weight," Brian explained patiently, as if there was no way I could understand something as complex as a hobby. "They're for fun." Then his expression changed, as if he were about to give me a present. "How about you keep going to the gym, and then if you meet your weight goals, you can take the dance classes as a reward? I bet it's not even too late to reverse your gym cancellation."

He smiled benevolently at me then, like he'd just solved all my problems. Maybe a year ago I would have done anything he asked because I'd been so grateful anyone could want to be with me—because I wanted to be this better, skinnier version of myself that he seemed to envision.

But something shifted deep in my brain, and while I didn't know exactly what it was, I knew I was *over it*. I was over the diets that didn't work. I was over the grueling gym schedule that left no time for fun. I was over hiding behind my friends whenever we took pictures. I was over shopping for print tunics at Blouse Barn.

I want to wear the clothes I want to wear, not the ones I'm supposed to. I want to spend my nights doing what *I* choose, not going to the gym and then listening to Brian's pointed remarks about my body while I pick at my frozen diet entree and stare miserably at the table. I want to live *now*, have fun and do fun things *now*, not wait for some distant, skinnier future that may never come. What if I wake up one day at fifty and realize I spent my youth on diet shakes and broth cleanses for nothing? What if I spent the rest of my years being criticized by Brian and gym trainers and my sister, all while wearing tunics I hated?

So I stopped.

And started wearing the clothes everyone said I shouldn't—crop tops and leggings and short dresses and over-the-knee boots—and I started taking dance classes for the hell of it, because it sounded fun and because I wasn't going to care anymore about being the biggest woman in the room or the one who sweats the most or breathes the loudest. I was going to live in my body *now*.

It was amazing—it *is* amazing. Yes, my sister still keeps sending me links to new diets and making sure my plate is smaller than everyone else's at Sunday dinner. And yes, Brian did dump me after it became clear I wasn't "taking care of myself anymore." But I feel freer than I can ever remember.

And if the price of freedom is being alone, then fine. I'd rather be alone than be with someone who will only love me if I'm skinny.

For good measure, I take another picture of my reflection, feeling a bite of satisfaction when I glance at the digital display on the back of the camera. Dark, loose curls. Cheeky lipstick. All of my curves on display.

I look good. Fuck anyone who says differently.

The wind picks up, reminding me that no matter how confident I'm feeling right now, I'm still stuck in the mud in the middle of nowhere with an angry thunderstorm bearing down on me. And no cell service.

With a sigh, I finally accept I'm going to have to leave the car here and try to walk to better service. I'm not looking forward to plodding back to the last sign of civilization I saw—a tired gas station five miles back when I turned off the small two-lane highway onto the gravel county road that led me to the mess I'm in now. Ugh, and in my cute pencil skirt, which had been perfect for "young professional meets Kansas farmer for a marketing campaign" but is not ideal for "size eighteen girl hikes five muddy miles in the July heat."

My thighs are already wincing, knowing from long experience the chub rub to come.

Why couldn't I have worn jeans?

Because I wanted to look professional, that's why. A grown-up girl with a grown-up job. Instead, I'm going to be the least professional thing of all—a freaking no-show. I was supposed to be at Caleb Carpenter's farm twenty minutes ago, and without a working cell phone, I can't call to explain myself. I'll just have to wait until I get to the gas station and figure it out from there.

If there's one thing Brian made me good at, it was apologizing, so at least I know I'll be able to work up the appropriate amount of remorse when I call the farmer back. So it will just be chub rub *and* professional embarrassment. No big deal. At least the rain seems to have tapered off.

Well, no sense standing here feeling sorry for myself. I grab the weekender bag I packed, throw in the camera, my wallet, and my phone, and then lock the car and start walking.

The cows have already moved away in disinterest. This situation is so dull, it bores livestock.

I reach a mud-covered wooden bridge over a swollen creek, and *bang!*—like a gunshot. Close enough to make me duck.

Holy shit.

I know Kansas farmers can be fussy about trespassers, but surely it's fine to walk on the *road*? Or maybe it has nothing to do with me and it's normal farm business to shoot off guns every now and then? Or maybe someone is hunting nearby? Do people hunt in July?

Before I can rationalize away the sound, it happens again, much closer this time, and then up and over the hill behind me comes a rattletrap pickup truck, sluicing through the gloppy mud without a single problem at all, easily shaming my little hybrid—even though my hybrid is barely a year old and the pickup appears to be held together with rust and fond memories.

It comes charging through the mud, heading my way, and for a moment, I almost want to hide. Not only because I'm a woman alone in the middle of nowhere and I have no way to dial 9-1-1 if I need to but also because I'm a bit embarrassed. Okay, a lot embarrassed.

Embarrassed of my car and my clothes and—even though I'm annoyed with myself about it—my body. Sometimes it feels like there's already one strike against me, that whatever happens, no matter what it is, a stranger will look at the situation and then at me and think, *Oh, well, it's because she's overweight.* There's a whole host of things people assume about my intellect and moral compass because I have a bigger body than they do.

That's the old Ireland talking, I remind myself. Potential for being murdered aside, it would be just plain stupid to pass up the chance for help because I'm embarrassed. At the very least, he may be able to give me a ride to the gas station.

So I stand by the side of the road and wait for the creaking truck to come closer, and it thoughtfully slows down long before it reaches me, so as not to splatter me with mud.

Up close, I can see it's an old truck—but not some classic Ford that belongs in a parade. No, this is a brown and white monstrosity from the late eighties with a broken tailgate and rusted wheel wells. The bed is full of an assortment of empty buckets, baling wire, and bungee cords. A tarp, shovel, and a dented toolbox complete the mess.

It rolls to a stop, and the door opens before I can get a good look at the person inside. A three-legged dog jumps nimbly down, barking madly at me but also wagging its tail, as if it can't decide to be happy or distressed about a stranger.

Three-legged dog. Truck that looks like a rolling junkyard. I'm expecting the man climbing out of the truck to be full *Grapes of Wrath*—weather-beaten and gaunt and probably in overalls—and I'm hoping he'll be the kindly sort of old farmer and not the scary American Gothic kind when he walks around the door, and oh—

Oh my God.

Oh my God.

He's not *Grapes of Wrath* at all. He's nearly six and a half feet of muscle and potent masculinity...shoulders stretching a

14

Carhartt T-shirt in the most panty-dampening way, worn jeans clinging to his hard thighs and narrow hips. Big boots, bright-green eyes in a sun-bronzed face, and a close-trimmed beard that would redden the inside of my thighs very nicely...

Oh God, now that would definitely be an upgrade from chub rub.

He looks to be in his early thirties, with the kind of straight nose and full lips that make you think things like *all-American* and *wholesome*, which makes me keenly aware of how *un*wholesome my thoughts are right now. Thoughts about his beard and his hard thighs and his hands, which are big and strong and currently flexing by his sides as if they're itching to do something. I don't see a wedding ring—or even a tan line suggesting he's ever worn one—and the bare finger is practically daring me to imagine sweaty, grunting fantasies.

I manage to drag myself away from my dirty thoughts long enough to realize the farmer is talking to me.

"Ireland Mills?" he's asking. Hearing my name out of this prairie god's mouth is disorienting, and I merely gape at him.

He smiles, revealing even, white teeth and a dimple sent from heaven. "I'm Caleb Carpenter. Thought you might have gotten lost on the way to my farm."

CHAPTER TWO

CALEB

I feel like I've been punched in the chest, and the person doing the punching is a five-foot-two girl with purple lipstick and eyes the color of a spring sky.

I'm suddenly a clumsy country boy all over again, even though this woman is at least ten years younger than me and clearly in need of help. I should feel pretty confident in this situation. Instead, all I feel is a dry mouth and a racing pulse—and an undeniable swelling against the front of my jeans—like I really am a horny teenage boy and not a man in his thirties who should know better.

But it's like that punch in the chest knocked all the sense straight out of me, because suddenly I'm thinking thoughts no gentleman should think. Like how I can see the heaving swells of her breasts under her fancy shirt, how those swells would overflow even my big hands and spill over my fingertips as her nipples harden against my palms.

Like how warm and soft her thighs would be against my hips as I nestled into them, how her ass would feel in my hands as I cupped her bottom and tasted the only woman I want...

The only woman I want.

The thought hits me like a second punch, and I suck in a breath.

This one.

Mine. Ours. Somehow, it's this city girl—the same girl I've been silently cursing all morning.

A friend of mine from my college days called and asked if I'd be willing to let someone from his company come out and take some pictures of the farm. At the time, it seemed dickish to say no. But as the day dawned and I saw how much work I had to do, I began wishing I was more of a dick to my old friend. I didn't have the time to spare to play tour guide, and I felt even surlier about it when the time for her arrival came and went and it became clear she'd stood me up for this thing I was only doing as a favor in the first place.

It took an unkind amount of time to even consider the possibility she might have gotten lost and not stood me up— after all, spotty cell coverage means getting disoriented in these parts happens often enough. After I had that thought, I pinned a note to the door just in case and then climbed into the truck, grumbling the whole time.

But now.

But now.

I owe my old friend an apology and a drink; I owe him everything. Because even though I've just met her, even though I can't explain it, somehow I know something has just changed.

Something I've been waiting years for.

"Oh, thank goodness," Ireland Mills says as I step forward, and she's got one of *those* voices. A slightly throaty alto that sounds like she's been in bed all afternoon.

In bed under me. Over me.

Between Ben and me...

I manage to stop that train of thought before my erection becomes fully visible, and I realize I've been flexing my hands unconsciously at my sides, as if anticipating the feel of her soft curves against them. As if I'm already itching to hike up her tight skirt and mold my hand to the shape of her cunt.

I could make her wet...

I could make her come...

And Ben—

"So then I thought maybe the gas station, because even if they didn't have a signal, they'd probably have a phone, and I could get it sorted from there," Ireland's saying. Greta, my dog, is still barking at her, and Ireland talks over her. "Do you think the car is truly stuck? Should I call a tow truck?"

Before I can answer, Greta decides barking isn't enough and starts trying to jump onto Ireland. "Greta!" I scold, but Greta is determined to smear mud all over Ireland's perfect black skirt.

I expect fear or disgust or at least uncertainty, but Ireland bends down and scratches Greta's ears. "It's okay, puppy," she croons. "We're best friends. You just don't know it yet."

Greta licks her face in agreement, and I'm going to marry this woman.

"No tow truck," I say firmly. "I'll take care of you from here on out."

CHAPTER THREE

IRELAND

Caleb comes forward, takes my bag, and tosses it easily into the cab of the truck, and then he walks back to me. I have to tilt my head to look into his face, and his eyes burn down at me with something that makes my nipples firm up into little pebbles.

"We may just beat the storm if we get a move on," he says in a voice that is all gritty, practical male. I want to wrap myself up in it and live inside it forever. "But I hope you don't mind if we make a quick pit stop first?"

"I—" I'm still trying to absorb the fact that Caleb has eyes like summer itself and they're currently looking at me like I'm the most interesting thing in the world.

He's probably just being polite and attentive, good manners and all that, I tell myself and my fast-beating heart.

I force myself to run through a flowchart of my options, and by far, going with this man I was supposed to meet with anyway is the best choice. If my phone doesn't work at his house, he'll definitely have a landline. And worst-case scenario, I could ask him to ferry me to the interstate motel thirty miles back. I brought a few days' worth of clothes in the event I didn't get all the pictures I'd need for the campaign in one go—and honestly, it might be nice to take a break from the hustle of Typeset and the endless judgmental nagging of my sister back home.

And who am I kidding? I want to be in a truck with the most ruggedly handsome man I've ever seen. I want to go to his house.

"Pit stop's fine," I say, flashing him a smile he doesn't return. If anything, his lingering smile from earlier slowly fades. His hands do the flexing thing by his sides again, and he stares like he's never seen anything like me before. Or, more specifically, he stares at my mouth like he's never seen anything like it before.

With a burst of self-consciousness, I wonder if he hasn't. Chubby girls in lavender lipstick probably don't pop into his life very often, and maybe he thinks I'm ridiculous or trying too hard or something like that, with the big smile and the crazy lipstick and the clothes that suddenly feel a million times tighter than they did a few minutes ago.

Oh God. Of course, it's so like me to meet the best-looking man I've ever seen and then he sees me as some kind of awkward sausage. *I* know I'm not an awkward sausage, but does he know that?

You don't care, remember? It's better to be alone than with someone who doesn't like you with the body you have.

Firmed with resolve, I renew my smile at Caleb. "Should I?" I gesture toward the truck. He starts, as if I've yanked him out of some deep and important reverie.

"Yes, of course." He walks over to the passenger side with

me—Greta following us with her hopping three-legged gait—and opens the door. "Careful of the step. It's a big one."

Wanting to seem capable and strong, I ignore his offered hand and make to climb into the truck. Except he was right—the step *is* big—and I forget how tight the pencil skirt is. When I lift my foot to pull myself up into the cab, the skirt manages to hike itself up to my thighs *and* hamper my balance, and I'm falling backward. For a horrible, humiliating half second, I'm falling with my skirt up to my ass, I'm going to land in the mud, and it's going to be so fucking embarrassing, especially after I made such a show of not needing his help. And then he'll think I'm a *clumsy* awkward sausage on top of it all...

I brace myself for the fall and the ensuing humiliation, but neither comes. The moment I actually totter backward, Caleb catches me with a quick arm around my waist and a big hand on my—oh holy fuck.

His hand is on my ass. My almost bare ass, and because the skirt has worked its way up so high, the ends of his fingers are touching the exposed lower curve of my bottom. The arm banded around my waist is pure strength, and behind me he feels as solid and unmoving as a wall. A firm, warm wall made of swells and grooves of muscle and man.

I can feel every callus on his hand as he lets me find my balance, and then I feel the infinitely long second where it seems deliberately still, as if he's forcing himself not to squeeze my flesh, and that just makes my nipples hard all over again.

"Oh," I breathe out. "Oh—"

I can't remember being this turned on *ever*, and my body arches against his in unconscious feminine instinct. I want him to grind into me. I want him to bend me over the seat and fuck me until I see stars.

"Easy there," he finally rumbles, and with my back to his chest, I can feel the words moving through him and into me. And then like it's nothing, he lifts me up into the truck, handing me up into the seat, making sure I'm settled before his hands leave my body.

My heart is beating so hard I think it might leave my chest.

I have a brief flash of the time Brian and I went horseback riding on a date. I held out a hand to him, hoping he'd help me dismount, and he laughed at me. *Laughed.*

I'd flushed bright red. I didn't expect him to twirl me off the horse like a cartoon prince or anything, but surely it wasn't too much to ask for help? Surely even big girls deserve a steadying arm?

But Caleb—Caleb easily caught all two-hundred-odd pounds of me without so much as a grunt of complaint and then placed me as carefully in the seat as he would a stack of china teacups.

I turn to him to give him my thanks—thanks laden with possibly too much emotion from this dumb Brian baggage I have—but the words die in my throat when I see Caleb's face. His sensuous mouth looks tense and grim, and there are new lines around his eyes, as if he's experiencing some kind of strain. His hands are restless at his sides again, and he won't meet my gaze.

Immediately I panic that it was the effort of getting me in the truck, and I have to swallow back a dumb apology. But for what? For having a body? For being silly enough to try to climb into a truck in a pencil skirt?

No. *New Ireland.*

Instead, I just give him a "Thank you!" and he nods curtly, shutting the door after making sure my feet are safely inside, and then he walks around to the driver's door.

Greta hops in first, settling herself in a heap between us, and Caleb grates out a "Buckle in, please," not looking at me the entire time.

Clumsy awkward sausage. I knew it.

But I don't need his approval, even if he is only the second man in my life to touch my ass. Even if he is some kind of wholesome, all-American sex god. I lift my chin and stare out the windshield, which is smeared slightly with mud, and try to adjust my feet around all the stuff he has in the passenger-side floorboard.

Caleb starts the truck and then sees me trying to move my feet. A faint blush appears above the line of his beard, on his model-like cheekbones. "Uh, sorry about all this stuff," he mumbles, reaching over to move a brown paper bag that's full of...mason jars?

I peer inside. "Starting a pickle collection?"

The flush grows deeper. "It's a gift. From a friend."

A friend...like a lady friend? Maybe out in these parts, jars of pickles are some kind of flirtatious overture? Or maybe they're way past flirtation, and this lady friend likes to send him home after a long, sweaty night with plenty of sustenance. Because nights with him *would* be long and sweaty, I can tell just from looking at him.

"Is this an old laptop?" I ask, trying to shift a second

brown paper bag with an old Dell inside, along with more mason jars of pickles and jams. The bag's got a logo printed on the side from a chain grocery store that's been closed for at least a decade—at least in the city. Maybe out here there's still a franchise open.

"The laptop is something my roommate repaired, and I'm returning it to a friend," Caleb says. "She's terrible with tech stuff."

Aha, so there is a *she*.

I don't know why this rankles so much, but it does. I frown as I finish moving the bag, which reveals a scuffed center console, and I give out an involuntary yelp.

Caleb startles at my noise and flings his arm across me, as if to stop me from going through the windshield—even though we aren't moving yet. "What is it?" he asks, alarmed.

"Th-There's bullets!" I manage to point to the center console, which has *bullets* just rolling around in there with a pack of gum and a small flashlight. I don't think I've ever even *seen* bullets in real life, not even once. Who even needs bullets in their truck? Serial rapists? Serial killers? What if my first instinct was right, and Caleb is actually going to kill me here in the middle of nowhere?

My squeamishness seems to confuse him. "Yes," he says slowly, "those are bullets." He says it in a voice like *what else would they be?*

"But why are they in your car?" I ask a little wildly.

Caleb tilts his head, his confusion growing into distinct amusement. "For the rifle mounted under your seat."

I nearly jump out of the seat. "There's a gun underneath me right now?"

"Relax," he says, barely keeping the laughter out of his voice. "It's not loaded."

"But...why? Do you use it"—I drop my voice into what I hope is my best serial-killer-soothing voice—"on people?"

He laughs, the rich sound filling the cab as he puts the truck into drive. "It's my varmint rifle, peach."

Peach?

Is he calling me *peach*?

"Varmint rifle?" I probe, deciding to leave peach where it is until I decide how I feel about it.

"For coyotes and foxes," he says a bit more seriously, his eyes casting around the surrounding fields as the truck works its way over the bridge and up to the distant county road. "They come after the chickens. Sometimes the coyotes will even give the cows trouble. Or they hassle Greta." He scowls as he says it, and I get the feeling he'd never forgive an animal for coming after his Greta-dog.

"Oh," I say. "But can't you just chase them off?"

Another laugh, and he's so handsome when he laughs that I have to look away. "No. They'll just keep coming back. And I'm not going to lose any of my animals because those pests are hungry."

The proprietary bent in his tone is so natural, so easy, and I can't decide why that turns me on. Is it the certainty? The strength?

Is it the sound of a male determined to protect what's his?

"There's a .410 shotgun under your seat too," he says all casual-like. "But that's for snakes."

"Snakes?" I ask, going pale because he's said the one

word that can scare me more than *gun*. Oh God, if I'd known there would be snakes out here, I would have been way more terrified to be stranded!

"Okay, maybe the guns are okay," I grudgingly admit, because I don't like the idea of sitting on lethal weapons, but I like snakes even less.

Caleb chuckles, turning the truck onto a gravel road, and everything leaves my mind save for the way his hands look on the steering wheel. Big and rough and capable.

The turn points us right at the encroaching line of the storm, and I see lightning flickering in the distance. Caleb gives a sigh.

"Fucking storm," he says under his breath. Then, "Here's our pit stop. It'll just take a minute."

We're pulling into a long driveway—although "driveway" feels like an almost luxurious term, given that it's a dirt track with weeds growing up the middle and plenty of long grass along the sides. A low-slung white bungalow comes into view, all the windows covered with old-fashioned aluminum awnings. Several wooden outbuildings surround the house, gray and tired looking, and a gleaming twenty-year-old Cadillac nestles close to the house. A windmill spins in brisk, dizzy circles, and a couple of acres away, I see the slow nodding head of an oil drill.

"Is this your friend's house?" I ask, wondering if this is pickle lady.

"Yep," Caleb answers, throwing the truck into park and opening the door. Greta hops over his lap and is off like a shot, racing around the house like she's being chased. "Mrs. Parry sometimes has ducks wandering up from her pond," he says by way of explanation for Greta's bolt for freedom, but I stop at *Mrs. Parry.*

Mrs. Parry?

Surely that can't be the name of a lover—

The screen door of the house goes *whirr-BANG* as it opens and then slams shut behind an old woman in buttercup-yellow polyester pants and a white top with matching yellow flowers. Caleb gets out of the car and walks over to hug the woman—presumably Mrs. Parry—and gives her a kiss on the cheek. He's so much taller than her shrunken frame that he has to bend down considerably to do it.

"Now, what's this?" she asks, pulling away from him and eyeing me with some amusement as I climb carefully out of the truck and join them. "Caleb, have you found yourself a sweetheart?"

"Well, I—"

To my surprise, Caleb is stammering a little.

Mrs. Parry is already turning toward me and extending her hand. I take it and sense her approval of my firm grip. She makes no secret of how she appraises me, looking from my muddy flats all the way up to my lavender lipstick and windblown hair. She may be wearing a matching polyester set, but her eyes are still sharp, and I get the feeling not much gets past her.

I open my mouth to explain I'm just here to take pictures, but she interrupts me.

"She's a good, sturdy one," the woman says with a nod. "You and Ben did well."

Sturdy? I want to give a huff at that, but then my brain catches on the name *Ben*. Who's Ben? Why would she mention a Ben when she's sizing me up for suitability as Caleb's woman?

Also why am I even wondering this? Why am I even letting her talk about this when I am absolutely not Caleb's woman, or this mysterious Ben's?

"I'm Ireland Mills," I say as our hands finally part. "I came out to take some pictures of Caleb's farm for a client."

"Oh," Mrs. Parry says, and there's a real look of disappointment on her face. Real enough that I forgive her for calling me sturdy. "Well, then. I guess you'll still need some food, Caleb."

"No, ma'am," Caleb insists. "This morning, Mrs. Harthcock sent home more food than I know what to do with, and I—"

"Nonsense." Mrs. Parry is already bustling back toward the house. "You and Ben are growing boys still."

"—don't even like pickles," Caleb finishes his sentence in mumbled defeat as we watch Mrs. Parry disappear back inside. "You should see our pantry," he says, looking over at me. "It's *filled* with mason jars."

"'Our' pantry?" I ask. "Is this the Ben she was talking about?"

"Yes. My roommate." He looks like he wants to say more but doesn't know what he should say. He looks...uncomfortable.

A thought clicks into place.

Oh.

I guess I'm too used to how things are back home in Kansas City, because I should have picked up on the clues earlier. *Roommate* might very well be what a hunky farmer calls his boyfriend out in the Kansas countryside.

I feel a retroactive rush of embarrassment at how much I've been privately lusting after him. And embarrassment on his behalf that Mrs. Parry thought I was his girlfriend.

"And the pickles and the computer," I ask, looking for something to move me past this awkward realization. "That's from another lady like Mrs. Parry?"

He seems relieved at the change of subject. So am I.

"That's right. Mrs. Harthcock and Mrs. Parry got left all sorts of land when their husbands died. Some of it they sold, but the rest they rent out—to me."

"So you farm their land?"

Caleb does this very attractive squint thing where he looks out over the Parry fields. It's so unstudied and honest, and despite the *roommate* situation, something about it makes my toes curl in my flats, makes my belly clench low. There's so much strength in it, so little fear of hard work and dirt, and I've never seen anything like it. It's potent as hell.

"It's a touch more complicated than that, but that's the gist of it, yeah. I rent the land from them and farm it, since their kids aren't interested in the business."

"Is that what you're here for right now?" I ask, nodding toward the house where we can see Mrs. Parry moving behind the windows. "Farm business?"

More squinting—this time at the storm. "I like to check on them before the big storms roll in. There's a siren down in Holm," he says, naming the nearest town about four miles off. "And another at the intersection of the county road and

Highway 50. But they can be hard to hear if the wind really gets up, so I like to make sure they have their weather radios and flashlights and fresh batteries. Mrs. Parry has a basement, but Mrs. Harthcock only has a cellar, and she has trouble lifting the door sometimes, so I come by and open it for her. Just in case the storm gets serious."

I stare at him for a moment, absorbing the fact that Caleb is not only handsome as hell, polite, and endearingly direct, but that he also takes time out of his day to go check on nearby widows. It's like he came out of some Perfect Man machine.

His roommate is a very lucky man.

Caleb notices me staring at him, and he gives me an easy smile, although his hands are back to that restless flexing again. And that's the moment Mrs. Parry emerges with a bag of jars, gives me a fond hug as if we've known each other for years, and lets Caleb kiss her on the cheek.

"I know the drill, son," she says as he's opening his mouth to say something. "I've got the weather radio on full volume and an arsenal of flashlights at the ready. Now you go tend to your work and let me tend to mine."

Caleb gives her a final peck on the cheek, along with a sheepish *you got me* smile that makes my pulse race, and then heads back for the truck. I'm about to follow when Mrs. Parry catches my wrist.

I stop and turn.

"You would be good for them, you know," she says softly. I'm about to gently deflect this, to find some way to hint to her that Caleb isn't interested in a sweetheart because he already has one named Ben, when she says, "It's more complicated than you think. Just keep an open mind."

"Mrs. Parry, with all due respect, my mind is plenty open, and I completely understand what's going on with Caleb."

The smile she gives me is a little sad and a lot pitying. "You don't yet. But you will. And I hope that plenty-open mind will stay that way when you do."

CHAPTER FOUR

CALEB

Ireland seems pensive when she finally climbs into the truck. Greta nestles her head in Ireland's lap without so much as a friendly lick first, and I find myself jealous of a damn dog. I want my head in Ireland's lap.

I want to give friendly licks.

Lots of them.

Until she screams my name.

I'm both irritated and grateful Mrs. Parry mentioned Ben. Irritated because I wanted to ease Ireland into the idea, because I wanted to seduce her to it slowly. Bracket her with me on one side and Ben on the other and palm her ass again while he kisses the lavender lipstick right off her mouth.

God. That ass.

The moment I caught her tumbling out of my cab with that madness-provoking skirt riding up her thighs...the moment I realized I had my hand on one of her softest, lushest curves—and so close to her most secret place—I nearly lost it. My dick, already thickening from the mere sight of her, went fully erect in less than a second. It was everything I could do to keep myself from pulling her tighter against me and grinding that hot column of flesh into her round cheeks. Everything I could do to keep from sliding my hand from her bottom to the luscious lace-covered lips between her legs.

Especially after that choked-off *oh* she made.

Especially after she arched against me.

Had it been some other woman, I might have. Because I wouldn't have cared what happened next. But I *did* care what happened next because I want more than a cheap grope with Ireland. I want to make her mine—make her *ours*.

Besides, Ben and I don't start things apart. Or finish them apart, for that matter. So yes, I was irritated when Ben's name came up, but I was grateful too, precisely because we don't do things separately. I needed that reminder, and it was as good a time as any for Ireland to learn there is a man named Ben who I live with.

I do wish I knew what Mrs. Parry said to Ireland before she climbed into the truck, though. She's very quiet now, and I don't know her well enough to interpret her silence.

I'm going to do everything I can to change that. Starting now.

"Your car," I say, giving a final wave to Mrs. Parry as we circle through the short gravel-speckled grass to go back down her driveway. "I can probably get it free now with my truck, but my concern is that it will get stuck in a different part of the road and you'll be in the same mess. It might be easier if we plan on coming back tomorrow or even the day after."

I steal a glance over at her, not missing the way her knee jogs slightly in agitation.

"I thought that might be the case," she says. God, her

voice is irresistible. I can't wait for Ben to hear it, to hear how smoky and breathless it is. "I noticed there was a hotel off the interstate—I could take a cab there—unless there's a place in Holm I could stay."

She sounds doubtful about the last thing, and she should, because Holm consists of four hundred people, a bar, a volunteer library, and more churches than you'd think a town of its size could sustain. But no hotel. There used to be rooms for rent over the bar, but Ben stopped that when he bought the place, because the effort of keeping up the rooms wasn't worth the one or two customers a month.

"There's not a place in Holm," I say, turning onto the road to head back to my farm. "And I'll take you back to the hotel if you'd like, but you're more than welcome to stay at the farm. I could talk to your boss and explain about the car and the storm if you're worried about the extra time away from the office?" I know Drew would understand—he's one of the most laid-back guys I've ever met. The kind of guy who offers to help you move a couch and doesn't even notice if you don't offer free pizza in exchange.

"I can handle my own boss," Ireland says dryly, and I get the feeling my offer might have been overstepping a little.

Well, tough. She better get used to being pampered and taken care of, because I want to make it my life's work.

And that's after *only an hour together*. Christ, I have it bad.

The road is straight and easy, despite the mud, and I risk another look over at her. She has this look on her face—a twist of her lips that looks self-knowing and rueful, a slightly determined furrow of concentration on her forehead—and it's the look of an impulsive person who's trained themselves not to be impulsive. It's the look of someone spontaneous and brave who's forced themselves into a box of stiff reserve.

I should know. I've spent the last five years unboxing Ben after his last deployment.

"I promise I'll keep you safe from the storm. And that you're safe in every way in my house."

She lets out a long breath, and it's hard to read her tense posture. Is she tense because she wants to say yes? Because she doesn't know how to say *no*?

"It's not that," she replies. "I just don't want to intrude on you and Ben is all."

I'm back to irritated with Mrs. Parry.

"It's no intrusion, I promise. We've got a guest bedroom—shame not to use it when it's called for." It would be a shame to have her sleeping in the guest room instead of mine, but I keep that thought to myself.

Come out of that box, I want to coax her. *Be brave for me, little peach.*

"You know, it *would* make the assignment easier," she rationalizes aloud, her knee still bouncing. "Drew really wants to put together something magical for this client, and the more pictures I can gather, the better."

I nod. Drew mentioned the client on the phone to me—the Kansas Tourism Board—and how he hoped it would be a stepping stone to even bigger accounts.

"And it will be more convenient this way, certainly..." She smooths that tight, tempting skirt over her soft thighs, and I can't help but track the movement with my eyes, wishing it were my own hands moving over her body. "Okay. I'll stay with you, as long as it's really no imposition?"

I can still feel the warm heft of her peach-shaped bottom in my hand.

"No imposition," I murmur, shifting in my seat to relieve the pressure on my cock. "None at all."

◆ ◆ ◆ ◆

My folks died when I was in college—my dad of a heart attack and my mom just a couple of years later from cancer—so the farmhouse has been officially mine for thirteen years...but hardly anything has changed since I took over the place.

Some of the equipment is newer, sure, and I have Greta-dog instead of my old collie Connor, but the house is still the same white, gabled affair—two stories of modest turn-of-the-century architecture, with a nice porch, big glinting windows, and a windmill right outside. I keep the land around it real trim and nice, and the same with the outbuildings and barns. All of it is freshly painted, and the grass is cut into a low green carpet nearly as far as the eye can see.

But it's humble for sure. It's practical. And I have to wonder what Ireland is thinking as we rattle down the gravel driveway to the house. Girl like her, with the slinky clothes and hair like silk, she's probably used to something more hip. Exposed brick and city views and all that. Here, the only view is of fields and the pond shining like a mirage behind the house—and the top of the water tower down in Holm.

I want her to like it anyway. I want her to like *me* anyway. And I think I get my first wish as she steps out of the truck and stares around her.

"Wow," she whispers, the wind tossing her hair. It also plasters her blouse against her body, showing me every place she curves and dips and rounds.

My hands are itching to touch her again, to shape over her body the way the wind is right now.

"You like it?" I ask, trying not to sound too eager.

She looks into the dark clouds crawling over the brown-green hills and then at the wind-whipped oaks and cottonwoods around the house. Tall, branching sunflowers bob and nod from the sides of the driveway and around the front porch. "It's beautiful out here," she says softly.

"It is," I agree with no small amount of pride. "Let's get you settled inside, and then I'll give you a tour before the rain starts for real. Maybe you can start finding places to take pictures. Forecast says it's supposed to be nice and sunny tomorrow after the storm blows through."

Ireland hums in agreement, and the sound goes straight to my balls. It's the kind of hum an aroused woman would make, and even though I know she's just stirred up by the pretty scenery and maybe the pictures she'll be able to take, my body doesn't care. My body wants to crush her back against the truck, shove up her skirt, and show her exactly what a country boy is good for.

I behave, though, and grab her bag from inside the cab and lead her into the house. She pauses at the porch to finger the petals of a sunflower, and I make a mental note to give her entire bouquets of them every chance I get—buckets and bushels of them if necessary.

Our footsteps echo across the old hardwoods once we

come through the front door, and I point out the living room, the kitchen, and the old-fashioned parlor near the front.

"Is Ben here?" she asks, sounding a little nervous.

I wish I could tell her not to be nervous because Ben's going to be head over heels in an instant for her, but that would require too much explanation. And besides, I'm not aiming to yank her into our life without her having the chance to learn about us. What Ben and I share is...unusual. There was never a moment we didn't know we'd have to be real clear with any woman about what we wanted so she could choose that unusual thing for herself.

Some women chose yes. Some women didn't.

And after Mackenna left us when Ben got home from the war, we almost stopped looking altogether. It seemed easier to spend the nights alone than risk that kind of pain again.

But Ireland...something about Ireland makes me want to try again. *Well, not just something,* I admit to myself as I watch Ireland climb up the stairs and then follow behind her. Her skirt hugs the rounded curves of her ass and hips and pulls around thighs that I know would be so very plush around my waist and hips. Heavy and warm and soft over my shoulders as I settled in to taste her...

And her hair hangs like some kind of dark magic down her back, the sway and swish of it as she climbs mimicking the sway and swish of her hips and highlighting the contours of her waist—which dips in more than enough for my arms to slide around to toy with her breasts.

It's not just something *about her. It's* everything *about her.*

She's got that body that makes me feel like a caveman, a

body that offers lush handfuls even for my big hands, a body that promises a warm welcome on cold winter nights. That hair and that playful mouth with its quirky lipstick. Her light-blue eyes and sultry voice.

But even more than that, there's something simmering under the surface of her that I want to touch, even if it burns me. She reminds me of one of the wild kittens we've got in spades out here—she'll play once she decides she likes you, but until then, all you'll get is quivering, wary stillness. But once you can coax her into playing, she'll play with claws and teeth and still you'll be grinning the whole time. She reminds me of Ben that way, although Ben's more lion than kitten.

Ireland turns at the top of the stairs, waiting for me, and I touch the back of her elbow to guide her to the guest bedroom, wishing I could touch more. The small of her back. The sensitive skin between her shoulder blades. Maybe even wrap my hand in her hair and pull until she gasps ever so faintly.

Ireland steps into the room, and there's still enough light even with the clouds rolling in that the dust is visible in the air. But the creaky metal bed has a fresh set of sheets and clean quilt laid over the top—it's not unheard of for Ben to bring home one of the town drunks to sleep it off here at the farm rather than in the sheriff's drunk tank—so we keep the room and the nearby bathroom pretty clean.

All the same, the room is fairly minimal—white walls, the quilt-covered bed, and an old dresser—with only the window and a framed cross-stitch pattern on the wall for decoration. There aren't even any curtains.

I fidget a little in the doorway, watching the storm-tinted

daylight gleam along the silk of Ireland's shirt, and I have the same discomfort I felt outside the house. What if this isn't good enough for her? Nice enough or new enough or—

"I love it," she says simply, spinning to face me. There's that smile on her face again, lips twisting up in some kind of private joke, like she's only just caught herself from doing something she'll regret.

I'd do anything to know what.

I set her bag on the bed. "Do you have something you'd rather change into?" I ask, hoping that's not rude as hell to ask, but surely she doesn't want to tramp around the farm in that tight skirt—as much as I wouldn't mind the sight. Or the excuse to help her over fences or up into the hayloft...

"I do have some jeans," she muses aloud. "No other shoes, though. I just didn't think..." She drifts away to the window, looking out to the grass and sunflowers and, farther off, to the fields waist-high with golden wheat. "I guess I didn't think about how it would be different," she finishes in a soft voice, almost as if she's talking to herself more than me.

It seems like she feels good about the different, not bad, and I give a quiet exhale of relief. Of course, I want her to like it here. I want her to like everything about here.

I want her to stay here.

Slow down. You've only known her for half an afternoon, and Ben hasn't even met her yet.

And if Ben doesn't feel the same as I do...then I'll have to give up this craving for her, this clenching urge to bring her close. He and I are a package deal and have been since the day I helped him pick up a pile of spilled crayons in kindergarten.

"Ben's sister sometimes comes to stay with her wife and kids," I say, "and we have some boots for her here. If you'd like to try them out, they might be better than the shoes you've got on."

Ireland gives me a smile—a real one now, not one of her secretive and slightly unhappy ones. "I'd like that," she replies.

"Then I'll let you change," I say, and then I leave her in the room, closing the solid wood door and resisting the urge to linger like a pervert in the doorway. I don't need to hear the sounds of fabric rustling over skin to know it will make me hard. I don't need to hear her small sighs and steps to know I'll want to hear those sounds every morning for the rest of my life.

So I go downstairs, put out a bowl of food for Greta along with a bowl of leftover chicken for the barn cats, and then I finally text Ben.

You still coming home this afternoon?

Thursdays are one of the days someone else closes the bar down, and Ben and I have a standing...well, not date, really. It's not like that.

I mean, it's not *not* like that either.

Yes.

It's a terse reply, but it doesn't bother me—Ben's been short with words and even shorter with smiles since his first stint in the Korengal Valley. One of the reasons Mackenna left us all those years ago.

> *There's someone here from*
> *Drew's company to take pictures.*
> *Ireland Mills. She's staying with*
> *us because of the storm.*

No reply from Ben, which isn't surprising. He would consider that text a conveyance of information that doesn't require a reply, not a lead-up to something bigger.

Which it is.

> *I like her, Ben.*

That's all I have to say, because when it comes down to it, I'm pretty simple with my words too.

Three dots appear and then disappear and then reappear again. I must have surprised him.

Finally, he answers.

Be there in an hour.

And that's as much as I'll get out of him until he arrives, I'm sure.

I put my phone in my back pocket, and then footsteps down the stairs make me turn.

And swallow.

Ireland has toes painted a bright, cute kind of blue, and a toe ring winks off her right foot. I wasn't expecting these adorable wild-child feet to come out of those fancy office shoes of hers. And then—holy hell—she's in jeans.

Lots of girls Ireland's size don't wear jeans, or at least

they don't wear tight jeans. But Ireland's got on jeans that hug every delicious line of her body, tight enough that I can see the tempting shape of her groin. And then she finishes coming down the stairs, and my brain sort of goes blank, white and blinded, like after a bright flash of lightning.

She's not wearing her shirt anymore.

Instead, she's in this painfully thin camisole thing—maybe what she was wearing underneath her silk shirt to begin with. I can see the lace whorls of her bra through it. I can see the slight shadows where her nipples are.

I can barely breathe. Between the tight jeans and the hardly-even-there camisole, I can visually trace every three-dimensional curve of her. The places where she's full and soft. The places that would give under my touch, under my body if I covered her frame with mine and slowly entered her.

When I was thirteen, we had to look at old paintings in art class, and lots of them had naked women. But not like the naked women you'd see in the dirty magazines a guy might steal from his old man. The women in these paintings were so *womanly*, with soft rolls of flesh around their bellies and dimpled asses and thighs. With the coy *vees* between their legs so plump and inviting. Some of the kids giggled when we looked at the pictures. But me, I couldn't breathe right, couldn't stop staring. After I raced home and did my chores for the day, I locked myself in my room and clumsily shoved my hand down my pants until I climaxed in a juvenile mess thinking of those plump pussies with their shyly pouting lips. Those navels buried deep in bellies you knew would be so soft, so giving, and those thighs and upper arms you could grab and grab and grab...

Ever since then, I knew. The way other boys had *types*—freckled or blond or dark-haired—I had a type too. Stretch marks are my freckles, and dimples and rolls are my hair color. I never worried so much about the why; it seems to me like men never have to defend liking blondes, after all. It's just my type. It's just what I like.

And fuck me, Ireland is *it*. Like every Rubens painting brought to life, with that plump shape between her legs, with her camisole revealing the places where her jeans can't contain her.

"You okay?" she asks as she finishes descending the stairs, her eyebrows furrowed a little. "You look upset."

Not upset, I want to growl. *Fucking horny.*

But I manage not to. I tilt my head toward the kitchen, where a back door leads to a screened-in porch and the spare pair of boots. After I find her some clean socks of mine—which bunch around the ankles they're so big on her little feet—and we get her into the boots, we head outside. I was so distracted by Ireland's body that I didn't notice she brought down her camera with her, but it comes out now as we walk around, with her pointing it at various things and then fiddling with the settings and muttering to herself and pointing it at the same things again. It slows down the tour, but I don't mind. I like watching her. I like how she looks in boots, silhouetted by distant hills and dark clouds, and I like how Greta plops down into the grass at her feet whenever she stops to mess with her camera. I like how the wind kisses the hair off her shoulders. I like everything about this moment, and if I had a fancy camera of my own, I'd take a picture too.

Finally we get to the old barn. Since I use the new, metal building farther out back for my big equipment, this one is mainly empty save for the tractor I use to mow and a single cow named Clementine. There's also a makeshift office in the corner—just a desk and a lamp, really—that I use to work on administrative stuff when the weather's nice. Or when Ben's in one of his moods and needs space.

Ireland stops by Clementine's stall. "This is your only cow?"

"This isn't a dairy farm, peach. We do wheat and some alfalfa, and that's about it."

"But," she says, peering into the stall where Clem is currently flicking flies off her back with her tail and staring at the wall, "I thought farms were supposed to have lots of animals."

"Here, we've just got Greta-dog, Clem, and too many stray cats," I say. *Way too many.* But I've never had the heart to do anything about them. Ben brings some up to the county vet when he has time to get them fixed, but it never seems to matter.

"Then why the one cow? For milk or something?"

"I get my milk from the SuperSaver." I laugh. "No, Clem was my Four-H bucket calf."

Ireland blinks at me as if I've just spoken in ancient Greek. "Four what?"

"Four-H—it's like—" God, how to explain Four-H to someone who doesn't know about it? Growing up, it had been just as much a part of life as church or the annual Holm parade. "It's a youth program all over the country, and I know they got lots of things you can do, but most kids out here did their plant and animal programs. When I was a boy, I had to raise a bucket calf, which is Clem here. Fed her from a bottle and everything," I say fondly, joining Ireland at the stall door. "She's plenty old now—older than most cows live to be, so she probably won't be here with us for much longer."

Clem huffs at that, which makes Ireland smile.

The wind is strong enough to make the wood of the barn creak around us, and outside the open door, I can see the first streaks of scattered silver rain. Won't be long before the storm's really here, and I send a quick prayer up to heaven that it won't tear up the fields or damage any of the equipment. Sometimes it feels like I can never get the weather going for me the right way—I need the sunshine but not the excessive heat that bakes the ground up drier than cornbread, and I need the rain but not the kind that comes with wind intent on flattening my barn.

Camera raised, Ireland snaps a picture of the scowling clouds framed by the door, and as she walks toward the opening, still snapping away, she becomes framed by it. Her curvy rear in those jeans, the dramatic inward dip of her waist, those bare arms...

I drift toward her without really knowing what I'm doing, my mind full of her and my body full of something hot and restless. She's just outside the doorway now, taking a picture and then frowning at the camera screen, and the indecisive rain has left a few plump droplets along her collarbone.

I'm transfixed by those raindrops on her skin.

You should ask. You should ask. Ask, ask, ask.

But I don't ask, and there's no excuse for it, and I deserve whatever hell she heaps on my head afterward. I know I do.

I reach out and touch a raindrop on her collarbone.

A breath stabs into her, and her startled blue gaze meets mine as her body shivers under my touch. I know how she feels—my own breath is stabbing at me, and I can feel every part of me trembling to touch her. Every part of me except for the one part that's rock hard and throbbing rather than trembling.

"Caleb?" She whispers the question and lets out a small puff of breath when I raise my rain-wet finger to my mouth.

"Yes, peach?" I swipe another raindrop off her collarbone, and another, enjoying the way the water then rolls down her chest and underneath her camisole.

Her nipples pucker into tight buds, and I think I forget my own name.

"I thought..." she says, all dazed and woozy sounding, "I thought that you—"

But she doesn't finish her sentence because I kiss her.

I kiss her hard and fierce, giving in to the hunger swelling up inside me, and I do what I've been longing to do all day and slide my arms around her waist and pull her body flush to mine.

I groan into her mouth the moment our forms meet. She's just as luscious and warm as I knew she would be, and my hard cock nestles right against her belly. Her full tits press hard against my chest, and I yank her even closer to feel more of them. More of her. Swallowing her kisses and moans all the while, demanding entrance to her mouth and then exploring inside the same way I want to tongue her cunt later—with flickers and licks and long, massaging strokes. And she opens to me so beautifully, arching her back into my hold and sliding her arms around my neck, kissing me back just as thoroughly as I kiss her.

My fingers twine through her hair, and I walk her back so she's pressed against the outside of the barn, raising my other arm to protect her bare shoulders from the rough wood. And then I really kiss her, pressing her hard against the wall, making her feel how tall and strong I am, making her feel how hard I ache for her. I slip a thigh between her legs, and she shudders at the contact against her pussy, rocks against me, and gasps into my mouth.

I drop my mouth from hers to the point of her chin and then up her jawline to her ear.

"What was it, peach?" I ask her as I nibble on her earlobe.

"What...what was what?" she asks hazily, still rocking against my thigh.

"You said before that you thought something about me, but you didn't say what."

"Oh," she breathes with a little laugh. "It seems silly now. Forget about it."

I've got my face in her neck now, and shit, she smells so good. Like flowers and all sorts of expensive womanly things. The kind of smell that makes you think of stores that have pianos and chandeliers inside them. "Tell me, Ireland," I say, nipping at her neck and then licking it until she shivers. "Say it."

I don't want her to censor herself around me. I don't want to be a reason for that twisting, self-mocking smile, and I don't want to be a reason for her to bite back what she really wants to say. Ever, and that means starting now.

She sighs happily at my attentions to her neck and then admits, "I thought you and Ben were a couple."

I stop.

Freeze, really.

And pull away.

She lets out a wrecked exhale as I do, as if it pains her to be separated from my body. Which, same. My own body is pulsing and aching and screaming to be back against hers. My mouth is lonely, and my thigh is cold without the hot weight of her cunt on it.

But still I pull back and run a hand through my hair. "Shit," I mumble.

She blinks at me. "I didn't mean to offend you," she says. "I just thought *roommate* might be some kind of euphemism, you know? And really, if you *are* offended, then I'm sorry because that's really narrow-minded of you—"

"I'm not offended," I interrupt. "Hell, Ben's sister is gay. Of course I'm not offended. I just..."

You just what, Caleb? Were about to ignore years of loyalty to Ben so you could dry hump next to a barn like a teenager?

Ireland is looking at me carefully now, and that kind of scrutiny plus her kiss-swollen lips and mussed hair is enough to make my torso clench again. Fuck, I want to kiss her senseless. I want to press myself back against her, but I can't.

Ben and I start things *together*. That means I need to wait for him.

"So you and Ben," she says. "Just roommates?" There's a hint of vulnerability in her voice as she asks, and I know what she really means.

She means: am I taken? Am I fucking around with her when I have no right to?

The problem is that I don't know what the right word is for Ben and me. We're not gay in the way Ben's sister is, and we're definitely not straight. But even *bisexual* feels incomplete to me, like it's one note on a piano, and what Ben and I share is a complicated but quiet melody.

A melody that needs a third person.

Shit, I'm no good at metaphors either.

"We're not just roommates," I tell Ireland honestly. "But it's not like... There's more to it than that." I run my hand over my hair again, feeling frustrated that I'm not better with words.

I'm a simple man. I like big girls, Kansas sunrises, and my dog, Greta. I like sharing those things with my best friend.

And as such a simple guy, I'm no good at explaining anything more complicated than a missing ball bearing.

"Oh," Ireland says, clearly still confused. She bites her lip, and my eyes fix on that spot like it holds the answer to every question I've ever wanted to know. "So this kiss...is it a secret from Ben? Because I don't like being a secret."

A small flame of hurt shines in her eyes, and I realize she's been someone's secret before. I wish I could find whoever it is and wring their neck, but I set that aside for now. I touch her chin and lift her face to mine so I can look her in the eyes. "It's not a secret, I promise. What I feel for you isn't a secret either; Ben already knows. But he and I—well, maybe it's just easier to explain when he gets here."

"Try me now," she says stubbornly, but at that moment a huge gust of wind catches the barn door on the other side, slamming it back against the wall with an ominous crack. More raindrops slice through the air, and I drop a kiss on her forehead.

"Gotta batten down the barn," I say. "And bring some stuff inside from the office. I promise, Ben will be here soon and we'll talk through everything, but until then, you should go inside the house and get you and your camera out of the rain."

I think she wants to argue more, but the racing wind makes it near impossible to argue, and she looks like she knows it. And I can tell from the way her hand tightens around her camera that she has very little interest in discovering how waterproof it is. With a frustrated shake of her head, she heads back to the house, Greta following at her heels without so much as a goodbye tail wag for me.

And even through the rain, I can still see the hypnotic denim-covered sway of Ireland's peach-shaped ass. God, what it would be like to peel those wet jeans off her.

Ben can't get here soon enough.

CHAPTER FIVE

IRELAND

I should be pissed, but when I get inside the storm-dark house, I only feel confused. Aroused. Achy in a way I never felt with Brian...or anyone else, for that matter. I stand there for a moment, unsure of what to do, simply watching the rain coming down in front of the porch. And then I turn back to the barn. I see Caleb outside, the mouthwateringly huge muscles in his shoulders and back straining as he struggles to close the barn door against the wind.

Jesus, everything about him. Those broad shoulders and sculpted arms, those flat abs and that thick erection I can still feel against my belly. It stretched all the way to his hip, a massive monster, and it wanted me.

I wanted it.

And then there's the way he touched and looked at me—all lust and grabbing and possessive. I've never been touched like that, like someone couldn't get enough of my body, and the parts of my body that Brian always avoided—hell, the parts I avoid touching myself—Caleb put his hands all over. He cupped my hips and slid his hands over the places where my waist turned into the soft convexity of my belly. He ran his hands over my ass *and* my thighs. His palm flexed against the parts of my back where my bra dug into my skin. And the whole time, I felt nothing from him but hot, throbbing desire.

This is bonkers, right? This whole thing. And yet it doesn't feel crazy at all. It feels necessary. Natural. The kiss and this hot longing I have in the aftermath. I try to remind myself that I started the day wanting to be professional, that technically this is a work trip, that Caleb is my boss's friend.

That it's unseemly to need to fuck under these conditions.

But watching Caleb in his wet T-shirt as he wrestles against the wind... Well, I'm willing to set aside professional seemliness just this once. After all, isn't it like a known fact that men fuck on business trips all the time? Why not me? If I'm single and Caleb and Ben are...well, whatever version of single exists for them?

Outside, the barn door is finally closed, and I watch Caleb go around the side to where I'm guessing the smaller door is, the one close to his rustic office setup. He said he had things to gather. He said Ben would be here soon.

I don't want to wait. Not for explanations and not for fixing the coiling need at the apex of my thighs.

It's more complicated than you think, Mrs. Parry said.

Well, it is certainly shaping up to be that.

I push open the door, and Greta looks up from her bed near the wood-burning stove, glances at the rain-soaked world outside, and lays her head back down, as if to say *thanks, but no thanks*. With a smile, I head out into the rain, cutting a breathless and wet jog across the short grass to the barn, having to circle around the long way to find the small door. It's propped open, and the growing roar of the rain is enough to mask my footsteps as I come inside.

And I thank God for that the minute my eyes adjust to the dim light inside the barn, because Caleb is standing slightly angled away from me with his jeans hanging open around his hips, the muscles in his arms bunching as he strokes and pumps at his straining cock.

Sweet merciful Jesus, the man is *big*. Long enough that the swollen head moves out of his giant hand as he fucks his fist back to the root and thick enough to make me swallow in a combination of lust and *oh shit*, because taking that part of him inside me would be a feat in itself.

The taut flex of his hips and the top of his ass where it peeks above his slackened belt is just the garnish on this masculine feast in front of me, and if I thought I was wet and aroused before, it's nothing like *now*. Now, when my nipples actually hurt they're so hard and I can feel the emptiness in my core like a living, keening thing.

I creep around the corner into an empty stall so I can stay hidden in case he turns—which is wrong. It's so wrong. In real life I'd never watch someone without their consent. But I *felt* him as we kissed. I felt his hands and his erection and his insatiable hunger for my body. And he didn't make it sound like he regretted our kiss, only that he wanted to wait for Ben... so maybe he wouldn't mind that I'm watching?

Maybe he'd even like it?

Except then again, maybe he wouldn't? Because he *did* lie to me, and he's not in here waiting for Ben by shuffling stuff around his office—he's in here jerking off his beautiful dick without me.

And okay, maybe it's a little bananas that I'm hurt by that, given that we just met and it's not *exactly* like I want him to go *Clan of the Cave Bear* on me and fuck me right in the wet grass...but also it's not exactly like I don't want it either? Sex with my ex-boyfriend was lights-out, missionary, and always came with this weird philanthropic vibe, like he was doing me a favor by fucking me. But with Caleb, it was like I made him wild, like I made him hungry for more of me, and seeing him do something as brutally primal as beat his cock the minute I'm not around him is rather exhilarating.

So maybe he wouldn't mind me watching or maybe he would, but the thing is that I've never had this feeling before—this *power*—knowing that I've driven a virile man past all politeness and civilized pretending simply just by being me, and there's no way in hell I can walk away from it now.

Plus there'd be no walking away from it anyway, because it's possibly the sexiest thing I've ever seen in my entire life.

Which changes in a matter of seconds with what happens next.

♦ ♦ ♦ ♦

Heavy footsteps echo through the barn, and I nearly leap out of my skin when I realize someone walked *right past me* and I didn't even notice. The storm was loud and I was watching the delicious spectacle that was Caleb, and...yeah. Maybe I wasn't as alert as a voyeuring girl should be.

Luckily, the man walking up to Caleb doesn't seem to notice I'm here—I'm tucked far enough back into the empty stall that I'm probably hidden from view—and who would think to look in a shadowy stall for a peeping Tonya anyway? I almost wish he had seen me, though, so it would've given Caleb enough time to cover up his, um, activities. Because I have no idea who this man is, but there's no way he's not going to see exactly what Caleb is doing, and God, Caleb will be so embarrassed—

"'Bout time," Caleb says gruffly. His hand slows on his erection but doesn't stop, and he angles his body ever so slightly to greet this newcomer. Who steps into the lamplight coming from the desk, and holy fuck. Holy fuck. Holy fuck.

I'm glad the storm echoes and reverberates around the barn because the breath I draw seeing this man is not quiet. It's jagged and rough and out of my control. I can't help it, though, because this man is the perfect complement to Caleb's open, wholesome good looks.

Eyebrows slash over eyes so dark, they look nearly vampire-black in the shadowed barn, and a rough cover of stubble can't hide how *pretty* his face is—high cheekbones and a perfect jaw and a nose as straight and strong as any model's. Furthermore, the stubble only serves to highlight his painfully perfect mouth, which curls up slightly at the corners as if it was formed to do so. But nothing about his face looks happy, and if you mistook that curled-up mouth for a smile, those glittering onyx eyes would chill you right out of the notion that this man smiled. Ever.

Longish hair, dark and thick and tousled, frames that magnetic face, and it's paired with a body as tall and firm as Caleb's, though this man has a leaner bent to him—less bulk and more grace.

I breathe out again as it occurs to me in a clit-throbbing surge of insight that he must be—

"Ben," Caleb groans, his hand starting to speed up again. I watch, fascinated, as Ben leans against the desk and crosses his arms, his gaze on the other man's stroking hand.

"She must have you twisted up something good if you're out here like this," Ben says silkily.

"Yeah," Caleb says, dropping his head down. I can only just hear them talking over the din of the rain drumming on the barn, and I can't hear the sound of Caleb's hand on his flesh at all, which is very disappointing, as I think I'd like that sound very much.

I creep a little bit closer to the stall opening, hoping the two men are distracted enough that they won't see me peering out. Ben leans in a little closer, as if to give Caleb an order, and his voice carries over the rain, as if the words themselves are made of silk and can thread themselves through the raindrops.

"Show me how much you want her, Caleb. Show me how much you want to give her."

"Fuck," Caleb whispers. "I want her so much. I want to give her...so...much..."

His lips part as his hand pumps his cock faster, and his other hand drops to cup himself, and my cheeks burn with needy heat when I realize he's talking about come. He wants to give me lots and lots, and it's so caveman and so fucking hot. And even hotter is the way Ben stirs up Caleb more with his dark words, the way Ben ignores his own erection now straining at the front of his jeans.

"That's it," Ben coaxes. "Show me. I haven't seen you this

worked up in ages. Is this all for her? Do you want to fuck her? Do you want to push into her pussy and fuck her until you come?"

"Yes," moans Caleb. "God."

"Did you make her wet, Caleb? Did you show off this big, strong body of yours to make her want you?"

Yes! I want to shout from my hiding place. *Yes, I'm wet. Yes, I want him!*

Caleb's response is another low moan, utterly helpless, and a wave of lust rocks me back.

It does the same for Ben, I think. His eyes flutter closed and his hand drops to his cock, still caged behind his fly. He doesn't stroke himself or even palm himself properly, simply pressing against his need as if he can make it go quiet.

Unfortunately, nothing is going quiet on my end. The raw sight of Caleb panting as he pumps into his hand and the somehow-just-as-erotic sight of cold, sharp Ben on the edge of succumbing himself is enough to make me desperate.

I slowly work from my half crouch to a kneeling position and unbutton my jeans, grateful again for the storm, which hides the metallic purr as I tug down my zipper. I slide down the front of my panties and shudder the moment my finger grazes my clit. I don't think that's ever happened to me before. Normally it takes a fair amount of porn or several pages of a smutty book to get myself going, but now I think I could climax with just a few circles of my finger.

"Come all over your hand," Ben urges. "All over this floor. Like you're coming all over her cunt and thighs to mark your territory."

My fingers delve lower, sliding between the lips at the apex of my thighs and finding them impossibly slick. Almost embarrassingly wet. But I don't care because it's all part of this heady feedback loop: Ben voyeuring on Caleb as I voyeur on them both, all of us unable to keep our hands away from the places where we ache to fuck and be fucked. It feels as undeniable as the rain, as urgent as the wind. If I don't come, I might die right here in this barn, only mere feet away from two men who look born to screw.

"Yeah," Caleb mutters. His head falls back, his face tilted toward the ceiling with closed eyes and an expression of ecstatic agony, and then with a soft grunt, his cock releases a fountain of thick, white semen. Jolt after jolt of it, landing all over the dirty floor, and it feels like it comes forever, like his orgasm must have been pent up for years and years, because there's so *much*, and the noises he makes are the noises of a man who's been denied for far too long. And I'm so close myself, so very close; I'm close enough that I bury my teeth in my lower lip in preparation to stifle my gasp, that I brace myself against the contractions I know are imminent.

Out in the circle of lamplight, Ben watches Caleb slowly go still, and they both let out a long breath.

"She must be something," Ben says, the heel of his palm still hard against his fly. He's just as affected by the unfiltered and brutish sight of Caleb coming as I am, but he seems to have more control. Me, I'm on the edge of my own orgasm, my eyes still riveted on the sight of Caleb's unflagging erection. But Ben is still all cool words and careful, catlike posture. Only his palm pressed to his covered cock gives him away.

"She is," Caleb rumbles, still catching his breath. "I can't wait for you to meet her."

"Oh, I don't think I'll have to wait long," Ben replies coolly. "She's right here in the barn with us. Aren't you, Ireland?"

CHAPTER SIX

BEN

I saw her the moment I walked in.

It's a good hiding place, I'll give her that, and with the storm trapping the barn under a dark bowl of clouds and rain, I'm not surprised Caleb didn't notice her in the gloom. Although it's also not hard to get past Caleb. He assumes everyone is as good and honest as he is. That everyone will play by the rules, wear the right uniforms, charge from the front. He made a great football player... Thank fuck he was never a soldier.

But me—I was an excellent soldier. Staying alive in the Korengal meant expecting no one to play by football rules. It meant knowing exits and potential cover. It meant knowing where people were hiding and why they were hiding. Five years hasn't been enough to break me of it—I don't know how many years it will take—and mostly I don't mind the ways the army's changed me. It makes it easy to keep my bar free of brawls and assholes, and right now, it's netted me a gorgeous woman currently staring at me with a bitten lip and wind-mussed hair.

She hesitantly steps out of the stall, a flush high on her cheeks—one I know will be matched on Caleb's face. Thirty-three years old, and he still blushes like he did in grade school when a teacher would call on him and he didn't know the answer.

He tucks himself away, zipping up with an embarrassed rush of breath. "Ireland," he says but stops after only her name. Which I understand, because really what can you say when a woman you like has just seen you beat off? In front of his best friend, no less? I'm not sure how much Caleb has told her about how we operate, but this is a much more dramatic introduction to our dynamic than usual.

However, dramatic or not, I was willing to take the risk. When I walked in and sensed her presence, glancing over to see her completely enraptured by Caleb's unintentional display of lust, I sensed she might be into whatever else I threw her way. And sure enough, I can see the evidence on her body plain as day as she comes closer—nipples like little bullets under her camisole, jeans unbuttoned, a certain breathlessness over and beyond the shock of getting caught.

And immediately, I *know*. I just do. Even without Caleb already wanting her, even without seeing the real and throbbing evidence of that want, I know this Ireland could be *her*. The one.

The one to break the spell of one-night stands and empty nights. The one to see us as more than just a fun joyride or a novelty.

The one to stay.

It's not just her looks, which are gorgeous, or her body, which is perfect, lush and soft and jiggly in all the places we like. But there's something about her gaze, her bitten lip, that suggests an adventuresomeness under the surface. A wildness that's been pinned down and glossed over but that's ready to break free. I'm fascinated. Hooked. I want to crack that glossy surface and tumble down into wild delights together.

Ireland stops a few paces away and tugs on her hair. "Um, hey. I was just..."

She's about to lie. I can see it in her eyes, which are all tensed up around the corners and refusing to meet mine. But I'm not going to let her lie. The stakes are too real, and it's been so long since I've felt anything other than tired and lonely, and I've learned the hard way that being a three takes much more honesty than being a two. Even when it comes to the little things.

So I step forward, grab her hand, and gently lick at her fingertips.

"*Oh*," she mumbles, her eyelashes fluttering closed. "Oh fuck."

Responsive too. I smile to myself as I give the pad of her finger a little scrape with my teeth and watch her shudder. I can already imagine having her and Caleb in bed with me, both of them following my orders...

She realizes too late why I'm licking her fingers and yanks her hand back. Her cheeks go redder than ever.

I run my tongue over my lower lip, tasting the lingering sweetness of her in my mouth. "You were 'just' nothing, Ireland. You were touching yourself. You had those pretty fingers in that sweet little cunt, didn't you? Watching Caleb and me?"

She swallows, blinking fast, but her stare doesn't leave mine, which I like.

"I—yes," she admits in a rush. "I was doing...that. What you said." And then she lets out a little snort of shocked laughter, as if she can't believe she just uttered such a thing out loud.

I'll have her more than simply talking about dirty things before I'm through with her, but I take this as a sign she's ready for something different. Ready for us.

"You were going to lie about it," I murmur. I reach up, wind one of her damp tresses around my finger, and give it a tug. Nothing too hard, not yet, but enough for her to know that when I'm here, I'm in charge. The other side of Caleb's sunny, happy coin. The daddy to our fucked-up little family.

She opens her mouth, and I tug on her hair again. "No lies to us, Ireland. Not now, not ever. Got it?"

"Got it," she whispers.

"Good." My hand still in her hair, I walk her back until her ass hits the edge of Caleb's desk. "Did you come?"

"Wh-What?"

"When you were playing with your pussy. Did you come? Did seeing Caleb jerk that cock make you clench around your fingers, wishing one of us were inside you instead?"

Another swallow. I'm beginning to grow addicted to the sight of them—how they move through her beautiful neck, how nervousness flits across her face right before she decides to be bold. "I didn't come," she says. She bites her lip for bravery and then adds, "But I did wish what you said. That one of you was inside me."

"Or both?"

She lets out a breath. "Or both."

Caleb steps up to her, his own face still flushed but his

dick growing hard against his jeans again. "Can we touch you? For real touch you?"

"Oh God, please touch me," she half laughs, half begs. Then another small laugh of shock at her own boldness. "I can't believe I just said that."

I've known her for less than five minutes, and I can believe it. I can see the restless bird inside her fluttering to be free. I've always been good at seeing inside people. Letting them see inside me, however, not so much, but I try not to worry about that right now. I focus on the goddess in front of me with the red flush across her chest and the thighs unconsciously rubbing together.

I tug at Ireland's already-opened jeans just enough to slide my hand inside, pleased to feel the damp tickle of her intimate curls against my fingers. Caleb likes bare pussies, just like in the old paintings that had aroused him so much as a boy, but I like the secret of a woman's hair down there. A private thing, only for lovers to know the feel of. And hers feels amazing, soft and not wiry, gloriously silky. I run my fingertips over her mound, my other hand braced beside her on the desk and my feet crowding hers so she's effectively trapped between me, the desk, and the hulk of Caleb at her side. He runs his nose along the edge of her jaw, teasing her into letting out little huffs of anticipation, cajoling her into opening up to us.

We've done this so many times that the choreography is automatic, effortless, but the difference is that this time Caleb and I aren't just willing participants in some woman's search for a good story, and we aren't merely looking for the nearest consenting body to take the edge off our loneliness.

No, this time we are both shaking with the wanting of this woman. This time, the need to make her *ours* is exactly that; this isn't about fucking and then waking up alone again.

This is important. This is real. I survived four tours relying on my instincts, my ability to just *know* things, and I believe my instincts now.

Ireland belongs to us.

The moment my middle finger grazes her clit, she lets out a low moan and her head drops against my chest, something I like the feeling of immensely. Caleb is usually the one women go to for affection, the one they inherently trust, and it never bothers me. But for some reason, I want Ireland to be different. I want her to see past the parts of me that are cold or intimidating and trust me anyway. Trust I'll take care of her, keep her safe. That there's always gentleness behind the little cruelties I invariably want to give in bed.

I brush my lips against the crown of her head, smelling rain and something expensive, maybe the kind of shampoo you can only buy at salons, or perhaps some other, more mysterious product only those initiated into certain levels of beauty care know about. Either way, the combination of expensive and natural makes me want to kiss her skin until she's a wet, shivering wreck, but I settle for keeping my nose in her hair as my fingers go lower.

Wet.

She's so wet. The pleasing plumpness of her mound and thighs have kept all that wet heat trapped right inside her seam, and the moment I part her lips, there's slickness everywhere. The kind of slick that means a man could slide on in and have her coming in under a minute.

The kind of slick I like.

"Shit," she mumbles against my chest. Caleb kisses her neck and then raises his face to offer me a smile. A real Caleb smile, with a dimple deep enough to show even under his beard and with crinkles around his bright-green eyes.

My heart squeezes hard. The loneliness has been hard on both of us, but maybe on Caleb most of all. I can use loneliness like an armor, but Caleb's different—for him, loneliness will only ever be a cold dagger between his ribs, a slow poison swimming in his veins. We've known since college that whatever's between us only works with a third, but the years since Mackenna's departure have proved it time and again.

We need Ireland. Caleb needs her, and I need Caleb.

I just hope she needs us too.

It takes almost nothing to send her over the edge. I can't even imagine how strung tight she must have been from watching Caleb earlier, because it only takes sliding a finger inside her tight box to make her tense against me and then only a few rolls of my palm against her clit to send her fluttering around my touch. She cries out against my chest, and her hands come up to search for us. One hand fists in my shirt and the other hand fists in Caleb's, and my heart clenches again at the perfect symmetry of it. Her holding on to both of us, both of us surrounding her and keeping her upright as she rides out her ecstasy with my hand down her jeans.

My cock *aches* at it, with how sexy she is like this, with how perfect her cunt is against my hand. With how much I've missed being a three, and I mean really being a three—not picking up a woman for a night and then waking up with Caleb in a hotel room she's already abandoned before dawn.

I need to fuck. And soon.

Ireland slowly comes down from her climax, her body relaxing and her hands unfisting from our shirts. Her face stays against my chest, and I can feel the instant she goes from happily sated to awkwardly embarrassed.

I pull my hand from her jeans and tilt her head up to me. Her eyes are a darker blue after orgasm—something closer to an ocean than a sky—and I can see uncountable thoughts and questions swimming in there.

"Open your mouth," I say in a low voice, and she opens for me. I slide my wet fingers into her mouth, and she closes around them, sucking without me having to tell her to.

Oh yes, she and I are going to get along very well.

"Do you taste yourself?" I ask softly. "Do you taste how much you needed someone to fuck you?"

Her eyes dart over to Caleb, and whatever she seems to see there reassures her.

"Answer me with a nod," I say. "And no lies, remember? Can you taste how badly you needed to be fucked?"

Eyes huge on mine, my fingers in her mouth, she nods, and I remove them, satisfied. "That's right," I say. "And you still need to be fucked, don't you? You need to be between Caleb and me so badly. You need to feel two big cocks hard and leaking for you and you alone."

She looks like her breath is caught in her throat, like all those thoughts swimming in her eyes are just trapped, trapped, trapped, waiting to break free, so I coax her by leaning down and brushing my lips against hers for the very first time. She tastes like mint and lipstick, and her mouth is as soft as her cunt. I lick inside and then pull back to breathe against her lips.

"Be brave, Ireland. Say yes."

"Say yes?" she murmurs.

"Say yes to taking what you want. To taking us."

A little smile crooks her mouth. "You wouldn't be taking me?"

I nip at her jaw and then at that irresistible little smile. "Dirty girl. You know you'll be ours once you say it. So say it. Say yes."

CHAPTER SEVEN

IRELAND

It feels like Ben is asking me about something bigger than a roll in the hay.

I blink up at him and then over to Caleb, my heart racing along with my mind, trying to sift through Ben's words.

Be brave, Ireland.

You know you'll be ours.

Ours. He must mean that within the context of tonight. That if I go to bed with them, they'll be at my sexual service—not...not what my heart keeps tripping over itself imagining.

That there's more. That there could be so much more.

That these men not only want to fuck me but love me.

You're being silly, I scold myself. *And you're overly romanticizing sex. They must do this all the time, and you're just the latest one.*

It makes sense though now, what Mrs. Parry said. *Complicated.* Feeling the two of them touching me and kissing me, feeling their awareness of each other—it was completely different than kissing Caleb against the barn or watching Ben goad Caleb into coming all over his fist. Once the three of us touched, something new sizzled into existence. Something bright and searing. Something that took more than two people.

Yes, that's complicated. Different.

But however electric this thing between us is, however magical, I'm also realistic about what it actually means. I barely even know Caleb and Ben, so how could it mean anything more than just fucking? Besides, I'm very used to the idea that girls who look like me don't get swept into torrid love affairs with hunky country boys. That stuff happens to pretty girls. Skinny girls.

No, this will be sex, plain and simple, no matter what intense words Ben lobs my way.

I still want it.

Why not? Being invited to a threesome with the two handsomest men I've ever laid eyes on? Hell yes, I want that.

When I was a girl, I wanted to climb mountains and sail boats and go places no one else had ever been. I wanted adventures! I wanted fun! And right now, adventure and fun personified are staring me in the face, albeit in a way I never could have imagined as a girl.

Be brave, Ireland.

"Yes," I blurt out, taking Ben's advice and being brave. Being the woman that girl wanted to grow up to be before people started telling her she wasn't the right size for adventures and didn't have the right kind of body for fun. Being who I was before I started being the one to tell myself no—*no, I can't do that; no, people will think you're desperate or trying too hard or too eager to please.*

I've spent too long caging myself in, and it feels good to beam up at the men hulking over me with hungry eyes and big hands and emphatically repeat, "Yes."

♦ ♦ ♦ ♦

It's easy to keep feeling brave as we dart across the grass, the rain coming down in cool silver streaks around us, the wind gusting past in huge buffets that nearly knock us off our feet.

Caleb grabs my hand, his fingers so warm and strong around my own, and then he's pulling me impatiently to the back door as Ben follows behind us. When I look back at Ben through the rain, the wind whips his T-shirt around the tight muscles of his stomach and chest, lifting the hem high enough to reveal glimpses of taut, olive-colored abs and a line of dark hair that disappears into his jeans.

Unf.

We stumble inside in a rain-wet and eager mess, and then I'm pulled up the stairs by Caleb while Ben stalks behind us, his eyes glittering with dark promises I hope to God he keeps.

Caleb leads me into the first room off the upstairs landing, and I know immediately it's his. There's something so basic about it, so *honest*, with the antique lamp on a wooden end table by the big, sturdy bed and a framed aerial picture of the farm on the opposite wall. A Carhartt jacket hangs off the doorknob of the small closet, and a paperback mystery sits facedown on the top of his dresser, the corners curling up slightly, like it got wet at some point. Like he took it with him one day out in the fields and got caught in the rain, or maybe he left it in the truck with the windows down.

For some reason, this little display of carelessness seals it for me. I've definitely got it bad for Caleb Carpenter. He spins me around so I'm trapped in his arms with my back to his chest, and I see Ben kick the bedroom door shut and prowl toward us.

I think it's only a matter of moments before I have it just as bad for Ben too.

It's deep evening now, and with the rain lashing outside, the room is almost completely dark—save for a nightlight glowing dimly in the corner, which is a rather endearing addition to a grown man's room. The light gives a faint burnish to Ben's cheekbones and a deep gleam to his eyes as he walks toward us, stopping a mere inch away from me. I could arch my back and my breasts would press against his chest, and the realization goes through me like a bullet. Suddenly it's all I want to do, to feel my nipples raking against his hard body. To feel one man solid and warm behind me as I rub myself against another. God, even just the thought of it makes me shiver. Talk about being spoiled.

But it's like Ben knows what I'm going to do before I do it; with deliberate slowness and care, he wraps his hands around my wrists and raises them to my chest, and it's less about restraining me than it is keeping me exactly where I am. Keeping me from rubbing against him like a cat.

"You want us to fuck you," Ben says, and he says it like a statement, not a question.

I answer him anyway. "Yes."

Lightning flashes outside, sending his beautiful face into sharp relief and showing me the primal hunger stamped onto his every feature. "Have you ever fucked two men at the same time?" he asks in a low voice, and God, those words in that voice go straight to my core.

Dirty, delicious words.

Dirty, delicious man.

"No," I whisper.

Caleb makes a noise behind me, his restless hands squeezing at me.

"What won't you do, Ireland?"

My brain struggles with a reply—partly because Caleb's hands are busy kneading my ass and hips and I can feel my body responding with fierce, wet need—but partly because I'm not sure I understand. "What won't I do?"

Ben may strike me as a hard man, but when he speaks, his words are patient, if cool. "You say you want to fuck, but fucking is an entire menu of things, sweetheart. It's always better to know your own menu before you start ordering."

I think about this. "Like hard limits?"

"Like hard limits. But also soft limits or preferences. You can do as little or as much as you like with us, and we'll be happy however we get to have you."

No one has ever talked to me about sex like this before. I've had boys ask if it's okay to move forward, if it's okay to do more, but *forward* and *more* always meant some vague notion of everything, like if you're agreeing to sex, then of course you'd also do oral and everything else in between. Like the only real boundary is between everything else and intercourse, and after intercourse, even that boundary goes away.

It's the first time I've thought about sex the way Ben describes it, as an array of things I can pick or not pick, and the freedom it allows me is almost giddying.

But then I genuinely can't think of much. Until Brian, I'd

never gotten past some fumbling attempts at oral, and with him, our bed play was painfully tame. I almost *wish* we'd found some boundaries, because that would have meant some degree of exploration, of trying new things. Of being brave.

I look up at Ben, dangerous and sexy as hell in the darkness, and I feel Caleb breathing hard behind me, his thick cock brushing against my ass every time he exhales, and I seize on the impulse, on the adventure of the moment.

"I want to try everything," I say boldly. "All of it. Any of it."

Ben's hands tighten ever so slightly around my wrists. "All is a big word, Ireland. A very big one."

It *is* a big word. That's why it excites me so much. "You'll stop something if I ask you to stop?"

Caleb growls behind me, and I think I've maybe insulted his gentlemanly honor. But I have to know, and in order to know, I have to ask. "Yes, peach," Caleb says. "We'll stop."

I stare at Ben as he inclines his head in a polite nod. "Of course," he replies. "The very moment you ask. Or before the moment you ask, if I'm not certain you're into it."

"Then all of it is fair game," I say decisively. "There's so much I haven't done—so much I want to try. How will I ever know I don't like something if I don't try it?"

Ben's lips twitch. "How indeed."

He steps forward right as Caleb steps back, and he pushes on my wrists as Caleb pulls on my belt loops, and I'm walked backward toward the bed. And then suddenly both men are in front of me and I'm being pushed onto my back on the quilted mattress, and then Ben is crawling over me with predatory grace as Caleb settles next to my side. Ben's hair is long enough to hang around his bladed jaw and equally sharp cheekbones as he does, sending dancing shadows across his sinfully curved lips before he leans down and kisses me.

Hard.

I gasp up into his mouth, not prepared for the onslaught of his kiss after the rather gentle one he gave me in the barn. But I can tell by the way he settles over me, by the way Caleb groans at my side, that this is how Ben likes to kiss, with cruel pressure and deep, possessive strokes of his tongue, giving me no quarter. I can barely breathe, but I don't want to breathe, not if it means turning away from this kiss, a kiss that says *this mouth is mine now.*

You are mine now.

Ben breaks off the kiss to turn my face to Caleb, who kisses me just as deeply but more gently. More sweetly, though the subtle scratch of his short beard keeps it from feeling tame. It's like a reward for enduring Ben's punishing mouth, but if Ben's the punishment, then sign me up for a lifetime of being punished. I'm practically writhing underneath them in need, my body aching to be filled after Ben's claiming touch and then aching even more at Caleb's worshipping mouth.

Ben wedges his thigh between my legs as he lowers himself to his forearms to kiss me even harder, a look of dark pleasure moving across his face as my hips lift of their own accord to chase the friction. "Poor peach," Ben murmurs. "Isn't she a poor girl, Caleb, reduced to fucking my thigh because she's so hard up for it?"

"It's too bad," agrees Caleb. His hand drifts down to my chest, fingers circling one erect nipple, and even through the fabric of my shirt and my bra, it's excruciatingly good. "Wonder if we can help her with that."

Ben leans down for another kiss, and this one has *biting*. He nips at my lips and sucks my tongue and bites along my jaw. He sinks his white teeth hard into my lower lip, and I arch up into him with a cry, and then he turns my head for Caleb to soothe it better, which Caleb does with attentive licks and strokes and sucks.

On and on it goes—a kiss of darkness and near-pain from Ben and then a rewarding kiss of earnest passion from Caleb— one man leaving me wrung out and shaking and then the other man putting me back together again. Until I think I can't stand it anymore, until I think I might perish with the emptiness low inside me. Until I'm begging them shamelessly, with my pelvis rocking up against Ben's thigh and my hands clutching blindly at arms and shoulders and my voice quietly pleading against the rain, "More, more, more."

Ben lifts himself, and with some kind of wordless communication, he and Caleb both shift to peel my clothes off my skin. Ben is efficient, clinical even, but Caleb can't stop his hands from wandering over each new naked inch, and I'm grateful for the darkness. I catch his hand before he can move it from my sternum to my belly, a flush now burning my cheeks at even the idea of him touching me there. His caresses have been so worshipful, so eager, but will they change when he touches that part of me? Without the semi-smoothing barrier of a shirt or jeans, without anything between his fingers and my skin? My breasts and my ass and even my hips... They're the parts of me that are easiest to like for a man, I'm sure. The parts that could almost be like a Kardashian's body—sleek and flat-tummied, a two-dimensional hourglass.

But I'm not sleek. Not in my arms or thighs and definitely not in my belly, which is not two dimensional in the least. And it's stupid, given that Caleb has already pressed against me, given that nothing about my clothes earlier hid my body, but something about my naked belly feels more real and intimate than anything else we're doing.

I don't know if I'm ready to share it with these men. I don't know if I'll ever be ready to share it with any lover, come to that, but especially these two? As fit and tight and hard as their bodies are, how could they still want me if they know how soft and loose I am?

I guide Caleb's hand back to my breast, which is still covered by my bra, hoping to distract him from my belly, and he palms it with the awed happiness of a teenage boy, but I should have known Ben wouldn't miss it. I should have known Ben would see, even in the dark, the things I try to hide. He seems like the kind of man who's very good at seeing what people hide.

He also seems like the kind of man who's good at hiding himself.

Ben finishes tugging off my jeans and panties and then climbs back over me with glittering eyes. "All," he drawls. "*Any*. Those were your words, peach."

"Yes," I say with a dry throat, because I think I know what's about to happen. And it does.

Ben puts his hand over Caleb's and slowly pushes it down from my breast. Down to my belly.

I suck in a breath.

"You can say stop," Ben says in a voice that almost sounds indifferent, but in the haze of the nightlight, I can see the rapid pound of his pulse in his neck. He's aroused. He's edgy.

He likes this, I realize, and I realize also that it's not just the obvious—making out and now having me nearly undressed— but also him moving Caleb's hand. Him nudging me toward something that feels awfully like a boundary. Something scary.

He likes the thrill.

And...I like thrills too. Or I used to, and now I'm relearning how, and this is my first adventure. I can be brave.

I swallow and wet my lips. "I'm not saying stop."

"Good. Because Caleb wants to touch you here. Don't you, Caleb?"

"I do," Caleb groans, his hand flexing over my stomach, running along the curve of it until he reaches my navel. He even caresses the part where my stomach meets my hips and there's this crease I don't think a single other human has ever touched on purpose.

He touches it. Traces it. Follows it across my stomach while he bends down to kiss me.

"Caleb, I think you should take off your clothes now," Ben says in that bossy way of his, which isn't bossy at all. More like matter-of-fact. More like commanding. "Show off that big, strong body of yours and all the parts of you that want to feel her."

Caleb gives me a final kiss and then grins down at me, an irrepressible grin that I can't help but return.

"What about you?" I ask Ben, turning to look up at him.

"Any parts of you that want to feel me?"

There's a flash of something like surprise, maybe even pride, across his face, and his mouth curls up at the corners. "There are some indeed," he murmurs, lifting himself off me. And while Caleb undresses, Ben pops open the button of his fly and works his jeans open enough to free the head of his erection, which even in the dim light looks florid-dark and swollen. The sight of him in his black T-shirt and jeans, with just the tip of his cock exposed, is the lewdest thing I think I've ever seen.

I'm panting for it.

Caleb is disrobing now too, fully, tugging off his T-shirt to expose a body unfairly masculine and perfect. His shoulders and chest and back are layered with swathes of swelling muscle, and when he unbuckles his belt and kicks off his jeans and boxer briefs, I see hard thighs that invite salacious squeezing and a tight, firm ass that does the same. Narrow hips, a lightly furred belly, and a heavy erection that bobs as he climbs back onto the bed. He wastes no time in helping me remove my bra, and then he and I are both completely naked. And then there's Ben, who somehow seems filthier than the both of us, more obscene, fully clothed with his rigid cock pushing through the fly of his jeans.

"Now," Caleb breathes, giving me another earnest, bearded kiss, "are you ready for all of it?"

CHAPTER EIGHT

CALEB

Ireland arches into my kiss, smiling into my mouth. "Yes," she says happily. Excitedly. "All of it."

I touch her again because I want to. I have to. I don't think I'll ever be able to stop. Her breath hitches when I run my fingertips over her belly, and I glance up at her face. She has her eyes closed now, as if she's steeling herself for something. For my touch.

"Now that just won't do," Ben says silkily from above both of us. "Open your eyes, Ireland. Watch Caleb touch you."

She blinks up at him and then over to me, her breath still stilted and her face uncertain. But she nods. "Okay." She swallows. "Okay. Touch me."

So I do. I touch the pale skin where the underside of her breast meets her chest. I trace down the slopes that lead to the sides of her waist. I stroke up to the middle and circle her navel, sunk like a deep well into her body, and then I move down to her lower belly with its gentle swell. And then—fuck—that plump pussy, the first time I've touched it. My cock jerks up as my fingers press into the giving flesh, and I groan, dropping my head onto her shoulder. She's even better than those paintings, better than anything a teenage Caleb could have imagined. I roll my head down and start kissing a trail down her belly, nudging Ben aside so I can settle between her legs and kiss at her stomach more easily.

She gasps at every kiss, trying to shy away, but I don't let her. I don't let her roll to the side or try to cover herself. I kiss her belly button and the crease of the place where her thighs meet her hips. And soon I have my mouth where I want it: kissing along her secret silk curls to her pussy. Pressing my lips to the coy little seam hiding underneath.

It's everything I can do to tease her like this, to keep my mouth soft and easy and almost chaste as I kiss the top of her mound and then at the sensitive skin on the outside of her cunt, where her thighs join to her body.

Because all I want to do is taste what's mine.

I want to part her pussy and revel in all the sweet heat there, all the slick wetness that Ben and I have made, and I want to feel the slick, tight channel my cock is about to fuck. I want to feel the new place I'll call home.

And even though I already knew, her pretty little gasps and stirs as I finally kiss her clit make it clear: this is for real. Which means one night won't be enough by far.

The thought sends a surge of possessive lust bolting through me. I seal my mouth over her swollen bud in a savage suck that makes her cry out and has Ben giving a low hum of approval. Using my thumbs, I spread her open like the world's best butterfly, pinning her lips apart so I can explore her. Her delicate inner folds and the tight hole tucked up inside them, all of it glistening in the dim light. Even like this, I can tell she'll be the prettiest shade of pink inside here, the kind of pink a man dreams about when he's got nothing but cold sheets next to him and a shameful fist.

I tongue and lick at her, like a boy with a county fair ice cream cone, trying to lick it fast before it melts in the sun. And Ireland is indeed melting, all of her shyness from earlier completely vanishing as her hands wind through my hair. Her thighs are warm and restless, pressing against me when she rubs my back with her feet, splaying open when she braces against the bed and tries to push her pussy against my face.

"He's good at that, isn't he?" comes Ben's voice. It's low and coaxing and just the tiniest bit cruel—it's sin incarnate. I grind my cock into the bed at the sound of it.

Ben's always been able to do that to me. Stir me up more, make me crazy, just with his words. And knowing that soon he'll be talking like this while I'm pumping away between Ireland's legs, well...it makes it hard for a man to be patient. I roll my hips against the quilt as Ben keeps talking over Ireland's whimpers.

"He likes that cunt of yours, I can tell," Ben remarks. "I can see the muscles in his ass flexing, and you know why? Because he's fucking the bed, he's that turned on. That turned on just from tasting you."

"*Oh*," Ireland breathes out. Her thighs are tensing and her belly too, and she's getting close. So close.

Ben notices, of course. "You're going to come, aren't you? Because it's just so good to have his mouth there making you feel good? Can you feel his beard when he kisses you? You'll be feeling it tomorrow too, you know. You'll be Caleb's beard-burned little slut. Walking around in your pretty skirts with your pussy still swollen and marked up by him."

"Oh God," Ireland chokes out, falling total prey to Ben's words and writhing against my busy mouth. "Oh my God."

"You like that?" Ben probes, leaning down to run his nose along her pert chin and the apple of her cheek. "You want to be Caleb's little slut?"

"I—both of yours," she gasps.

"My slut too?"

"*Yes*," she moans.

"Then be a good slut and come for Caleb. His cock is full of come to give you, but it needs you wet and tight, doesn't it?"

Aw, shit. I'm practically boring a hole into this mattress I'm so fucking worked up now, and between Ben's words and Ireland's sweet pussy trembling against the flat of my tongue, I'm not sure if I'll even make it to fucking her.

"Answer me, Ireland," Ben says sternly.

I look up over the rise of Ireland's curls to see that she's cresting now, her entire body a tensed stretch of quivering curves.

"Doesn't it?" Ben demands again, reaching out and collaring her throat with a hand to turn her face to his. And that's all it takes—the combination of his filthy words and his hand at her throat and my devouring her pussy like I'll never get to taste a woman ever again—and she's right there, tipping over the edge.

"Yes," she says in a cry, and then she releases against my lips, coming with a final small slick of sweetness and a helpless arch of her back. I'm too far gone to stop eating her, though, lost to the taste of her and the feel of her on my lips, and it's

Ben who pulls me away from her pussy by the nape of my neck.

"Look at what you've done," Ben says to our girl as I reluctantly rise to my knees. He runs a hand along Ireland's thigh, and she shudders under his touch, her body still visibly trembling with the aftershocks. "Look at poor Caleb. Look at how much he needs you."

The three of us look down at my cock, which is enormous right now, standing out from my hips in a hard, angry jut. I feel an uncommon surge of pride about how big I am, and it only surges more when Ireland's eyes widen ever so slightly as she takes in my size.

"Big," she gets out in a throaty voice. "So big."

"It's for you, baby," I say, giving myself a rough, helpless stroke from root to tip. "All for you."

Ben presses a condom in my hand, and I find my hands are shaking as I tear it open. Maybe I came earlier in the barn, but that feels like another life, another world. The tough, familiar fuck of my fist can't compare to even the promise of Ireland's body, so slick and soft and tight. It's like I've never come before, never in my whole life, that's how fucking keyed up I am as I finally get the condom pinched and rolling over my engorged shaft. That's how full my sack feels as I finally move between Ireland's legs, like I've got a lifetime of semen saved up just for her.

Even in the dark, I see that smile of hers that hurts my heart—the rueful one that means she's holding something back. That she's telling herself not to do or say something, and it makes me urgent to help her let go. To turn that troubled smile into a real one, into a smile that only knows pleasure and happiness.

Ben catches it too and slants me a look. He doesn't have to say anything, but we both know I'm better at this than he is. I've been practicing with him for years, after all.

"Tell us, peach," I say. I sit back on my heels between her legs, and Ben does the same at her side, the head of his cock still wedged out from his jeans but his body completely still.

She blinks in bemusement, her eyes still glazed with lust and post-climax bliss. "Tell you what?"

"You wanted to say or do something, but then you stopped. What was it?" I keep my voice warm, keep my hands to myself, even though in this position I can see the opened petals of her pussy waiting for me and my fingers are flexing with the urge to trace her secrets.

Her cheeks darken. "Oh. It's...it's nothing. Just me being silly."

"Nothing's silly to us," I assure her.

"I—" She bites her lip, and it's so fucking adorable and sexy I want to die. "I was just thinking about how I wanted to grab you and yank you down to me. Like pull you on top of me and just make you fuck me across the bed." She gives a little laugh. "And then I realized that would probably look too eager. Maybe even desperate."

I growl and lunge forward, sealing off her words with a hot kiss. "I'm the desperate one," I grate out against her mouth. "I'm the one who's too eager. I'm about to come inside this condom without even going inside you."

"Grab him," Ben says. "Use him. He likes being used, don't you, Caleb?"

I grunt in response, too busy kissing her to search for

words, and she huffs out a little laugh against my lips. "So it's not too embarrassing if I want you that badly?"

Her voice is shy, and I pull up a little to search her face. "How could you even think such a thing?" I ask. "The only one about to be embarrassed is me because I'm not going to last longer than two thrusts inside you."

Her eyes shine up at me, and finally I get the smile I was hoping for—brave, bold, free. "Let's find out," she says, her hands trailing down my stomach to my hips. She grabs at my ass, and I'm done for. Done waiting, done holding on, done with everything that isn't fucking her until the bed falls apart. I dig my fingers into her hip to hold her steady, and then I wedge inside with one heavy, forceful shove.

And fuck *me*, she is even tighter and hotter than I ever could have dreamed. The squeeze at my head only grows more excruciating the deeper I push, until all of me is being clenched by her hot, silky grip.

She arches at the invasion, but I don't let up until I've got her seated on the full length of my dick and I can feel the intimate kiss of her pussy against my root. I keep my left hand at her hip, the right planted by her head, and I lean forward to give her another quick kiss and check in. "Doing okay?" I ask. I can hear how tightly strung my words are, and it's because my entire body feels like a rope that's about to snap. I have to fuck, I have to thrust, but I keep myself rigid and still until I know she's good. Until I know she wants to keep going.

She gives me a breathless nod. "More," she chokes out. "More now."

It's the only thing my body seems to remember how to do.

I give an experimental pump, which makes her cry out, and then I can't wait any longer. I need more of those cries, more of her tits bouncing with every movement, more of her body giving and yielding under mine. I drive into her with a flurry of raw and hungry strokes, craving more and more and more, needing to fuck and fuck and fuck.

"Oh God," she manages, her hands flying up to brace herself against the headboard. "Oh *fuck*. Yes, yes, yes."

Ben is nearing his breaking point. His hand comes up to grip the headboard hard, and his chest is heaving under his T-shirt as he watches me plow into my peach. As he watches her moan and writhe under me.

"Ben." She whispers his name, looking up at him, and he looks down at her with an expression that might look buttoned up tight but I know is anything but. His buttons are unbuttoning, and his control is getting loose and hot, and I haven't seen it happen in so long, and even then I've never seen him quite like this. Never this close to wild, never so primitive that I think he might break the furniture.

With a low curse, he grabs his cock and feeds the tip of it into her mouth. "Just the head," he grinds out. "Suck on the head."

Ireland eagerly complies, craning her neck to accommodate him, and I ease up on the pace so she can suck his dick more easily. All the kissing and all the rain has exposed the natural berry-pink color of her lips, but I wonder as I fuck her if she's got any more of that pretty purple lipstick with her. I wouldn't mind seeing it on Ben's cock...or my own.

Wouldn't mind it at all, in fact.

Ben keeps his fist wrapped around his length, only allowing Ireland access to his tip, and he mutters instructions to her. "Suck harder. Swirl your tongue and lick the slit—yes, just like that. You're such a good girl."

With a groan, I speed up again, hardly able to stand it. How fucking sexy the two of them look like this, how fucking beautiful Ireland is, how fucking good she feels around me. How much I want this to last forever and ever. How much I want to keep her.

Ireland moans around Ben's crown as I screw her harder, and I bend down to suck at one of her pert nipples and then the other, noticing how she moans even more as my beard scratches along the sweet curves of her tits.

"I love that you love my beard, baby doll," I say. "Is it the pain? Is it being marked by me?"

Ben slides himself from her mouth, waiting for her to answer.

"I don't know," she pants out. "Both? Both. Just...more. More now."

More seems to be Ireland's new favorite word, and I vow again I'm going to marry this woman as I bite at her breasts and she whimpers *more*. As Ben feeds her his cock and *more* is what she exhales when he finally lets her come up for air. And *more* is the final word she cries out before she comes again, contracting down so hard around my cock that I have to fight to keep myself inside her as she rides it out on me.

Sated, she eventually stills underneath me.

"One more," I say, giving her favorite word back to her. "Give us one more."

"I can't," she pleads, but I can still feel her body responding to my own deep inside her.

"You can," Ben growls. I move my hand from her hip to her clit, giving her grinding circles that bulldoze past her *I can't*s. She's moaning again, loudly, even around the cock Ben keeps pushing in her mouth, and then he says, "Suck it, sweetheart. Hard as you can."

The hand on his cock clenches as tight as the hand on the headboard, and I see the minute he hits the point of no return, the moment he finally releases. His entire body tenses, and he gives a low grunt, still aiming himself down Ireland's throat and giving her every single bit of it, visibly pulsing in his hand, and Ireland works hard to swallow it as fast as he gives it to her. And I think she and I are both so helpless in the face of his rigid pleasure, with his locked jaw and fluttering eyes and massive, throbbing cock finally getting what it needs. She swallows his last gifts to her and then comes again uttering his name, and then mine, and then God's.

I'm like a freight train, barreling into her deep and fast, a near roar ripping from my throat as I finally fill that condom all the way the fuck up, still pumping the whole time through. I can feel it in my thighs and deep in my balls and all the way up my stomach, and still I throb into the condom as the last of her orgasm pulls every single drop out of me and closer to her.

And then it's finished. We gradually catch our breaths, unraveling into an obliterated kind of quiet, where there's only the storm outside and our still-rough breathing.

Ireland reaches up for me with one hand, the other resting limply on Ben's thigh. And then our amazing girl laughs. Laughs and laughs like she's just gotten off the best roller coaster of her life and she can't wait to get on again.

And I think Ben and I might be able to help her with that.

CHAPTER NINE

IRELAND

We fuck again. And this time, Ben flips me over onto all fours and slides his huge cock into me from behind while Caleb fists a hand in my hair and guides me all around his cock. Unlike Ben, Caleb wants my mouth everywhere—every crease and groove and needy inch—and also unlike Ben, Caleb has almost zero control over his own reactions as I suckle at him. He groans my name like a prayer, his hand trembles in my hair, and even his thighs shake as I tend to his cock.

Behind me, Ben is a force of nature. Like the storm outside but potentially more destructive. He fucks me like he wants to split me in half, like if he fucks me hard enough, he can break me open and eat my heart. And I'll be damned if it isn't tearing me apart with how much I like it.

I've never had sex like this before, sex like my lover's life depends on it, and that's how both men fuck in their different ways. Caleb with the mindless need of a caveman; Ben with the cold grace of a predator. Between the two of them, I'm going to set a world record for number of orgasms in one night.

Between the two of them, I feel like the sexiest woman in the world.

Again, Ben comes with stillness and a quiet, nearly regretful grunt, and Caleb comes loud with hips bucking and hands grabbing. I smile when I think about those hands earlier today. About how they seemed so restless by his sides, flexing and twitching. He clearly likes having someone to claim and grab, and tonight that someone is me, and I couldn't be happier. After we get cleaned up and tumble back into bed, he spoons me from behind and palms a breast with one hand and my cunt with another, not to start another round of sex but with a firm kind of possessiveness, as if to say *these are mine*.

I love it. I try not to think about how much I love it, and I definitely try not to think about how tomorrow is going to bring the harsh blear of reality over all of this. The tawdriness of taking two men to bed—even though I feel nothing but sheer contentment and a smug kind of feminine pride right now.

I wonder how the men will feel tomorrow. Politely indifferent? Trying to get me out the door as fast as possible before I get any wild romantic notions in my head?

Or, worst of all, embarrassed? For sleeping with me?

Ugh.

I push away the worry and the fear and try to settle into Caleb's possessive embrace. He's already asleep as Ben settles next to me—not on his side but on his back so that he faces up to the ceiling, and there's something kind of intimate about it, looking at him while he isn't looking at me.

In the faint gold light of the nightlight, aided by the occasional flash of lightning, I can study the sculpted perfection of his profile. The proud, nearly aquiline nose. The careful part of his lips. The stillness of his forehead and chin—the stillness of his everything, actually, which makes me wonder how much practice he's had at keeping himself motionless. Inert.

But his eyes—those aren't motionless at all. They gleam as they move from the window to the ceiling to me and Caleb and then back again, betraying a restlessness, a cloud of hidden thoughts.

It both fascinates and depresses me, that cloud. That fog of mystery that clings around him and covers him up. I want to burn away his gloom and see him smile.

"Thank you," he finally says. The lash of the rain almost swallows up his words, but I hear them anyway.

I don't know if I like them.

"You don't have to thank me," I say. "This wasn't me doing you a favor. And I hope," I add, in a mix of courage and insecurity, "that it wasn't you doing *me* a favor."

He turns his head and gives me a sharp look. "It wasn't."

"Then why even bring *thank you* into it?"

He lets out a long breath, and when he turns his head to look at the ceiling again, his expression is unreadable. "Because tonight is the first night in five years I've even been able to pretend I could fall asleep during a storm."

It's a strange thing to say—even stranger given I haven't seen him react to the thunder at all—but before I can ask anything more, he says, "Go to sleep, Ireland."

I want to argue, want to fight off the wave of drowsiness pulling at me and ask him more about it, but it turns out Ben must know me better than I know myself, because I open my mouth to tell him he can't boss me around, and before I know it, I'm asleep.

♦ ♦ ♦ ♦

It's still storming and dark when I wake up, and it's disorienting, like I've slid into another world where rain and darkness are the defaults and I'll never see sunlight again.

Even more disorienting is the hard warmth enveloping me, the breath ruffling my hair, the huge hand cupping my pussy—but it's disorienting in the best kind of way, like waking up to find a dream is real after all.

Although the dream isn't perfect—when my eyes adjust to the dark and my mind unfogs, I realize the other side of the bed is empty save for a three-legged dog tucked into a circle.

Ben is gone.

"He always leaves," Caleb says sleepily from behind me. "Don't worry about it."

"Oh," I murmur, not knowing what else to say. What else do I have a right to say, really? I don't know Ben, and I barely know Caleb any better. I'm just a stranger in a strange bed listening to the rain.

So it shouldn't sting as much as it does that Ben isn't next to me.

This is all going to be over in the morning anyway. What does it matter?

But it does matter, it does bother me, and even though I want to be all sophisticated and casual about the fact that I just had the best sex of my life with the hottest men I've ever seen, I can't be.

This is just an inaugural adventure, I try to soothe myself. *There will be lots more. You're the new Ireland, remember?*

There will be so many other hot men in your future.

The problem, I realize as I drift back into sleep, is that I don't want there to be any other men. I want *these* ones. I want Caleb and Ben.

After just one night.

God, I'm screwed.

◆ ◆ ◆ ◆

It's the silence that wakes me for the final time, or maybe it's Greta's high-pitched whine as she paces on Caleb's side of the bed and tries to get his attention.

Maybe it's the strange light oozing in through the window. It's lighter than it was when I woke up earlier but darker than daylight should be and pitched in a color that makes me uneasy. I sit up, realizing what the silence is—no distant hum of the air conditioning or the refrigerator, no background hiss of plugged-in appliances. The power is out.

"Caleb?" I nudge Caleb's massive bulk, which is now prone and sprawled, although he's still kept an arm wrapped around my waist even in his sleep. "Caleb, wake up."

He opens his eyes right as the sirens start.

"Shit," he mutters, sitting up and wiping at his face. "Shit. We gotta get downstairs."

Greta whines in agreement, but I look again through the window and see nothing of alarm, really. A sky coffered with dark clouds, with a distant clear band on the horizon. "Do we have to?" I stretch. "It doesn't look so bad, and at home, I usually just ignore the sirens."

Caleb looks at me as if I'm some kind of lunatic. "We don't

ignore them out here. We're going downstairs."

With a sigh, I roll out of bed, making a face at my jeans still damp and crumpled on the floor. I go to my room across the hall and pull on a pair of shorts and a tank top, and when I come back out, both Caleb and Ben are pacing the small landing at the top of the stairs. They're both still shirtless, with jeans clinging to narrow, fit hips, and I mentally curse the sirens. I want to take them back to bed.

"Downstairs," Ben says shortly, and when I don't move fast enough for him, he takes my hand and leads me down the steps. Caleb scoops Greta into his arms and follows, and our little parade climbs down a set of rickety stairs to a stone-walled basement by the light of a small flashlight Ben holds in his other hand.

Caleb sits down on a threadbare rug with Greta in his lap, holding her while she trembles, and Ben hauls out a dusty storage container and produces some candles and a lighter. Soon we're in a circle of flickering light, and in my sleepy state, I can almost imagine it's still nighttime. That morning hasn't come, and with it all the consequences of my adventure last night and all the decisions that now have to be made.

Except morning has come, and the soreness between my legs reminds me very much of the consequences and decisions. I fucked two men, came more times than I would have thought humanly possible, and now I have to figure out how to extricate myself with the most dignity possible.

Well, after the storm is over, I suppose. Then the dignity and such. For now, I'm content to watch the candlelight on Caleb's big hands as he tenderly pets his terrified dog. To listen to Ben move around the basement gathering up various items—a weather radio and batteries and a bottle of water and bowl for Greta—and to the wind shaking the house above us. Even in the basement, I can hear the distant wail of the sirens.

"I wish I had my phone," I murmur. I left it upstairs in the rush to get dressed and to the basement. "I could check the weather."

"Signal's bad enough around the house," Caleb says with an apologetic smile. "It's even worse down here."

I sigh and lean back. It's both boring and weirdly energizing to be without my phone at a time when I'd normally be using the hell out of it, and it makes me hyperaware of everything. The way the candlelight moves across Ben's bare chest and beautiful features as he sits on the floor next to Caleb. The way Caleb's eyelashes fan across his cheekbones as he closes his eyes and croons to Greta.

The way neither of them are touching me.

Oh God.

What if this is it? What if this is the beginning of the inevitably awkward end? What if it actually began ending the minute Ben left Caleb and me in bed? That's a very telling thing to do, right? One of those actions that speaks louder than words—so much louder it's practically a shout?

I don't want you again. That's what it shouts.

I adjust my position on the hard floor, again feeling the ache and lingering sting in my pussy from being so well-used last night. At least I don't feel ashamed. I worried about that last night, before I fell asleep, that there'd be some kind of *good girls don't have threesomes* panic, but I don't feel anything even approaching shame. If anything, I'm a little proud I had such a good adventure with such handsome men, that I was brave, that I did something impulsive and electrifying without stopping or censoring myself. Every part of it was good, and even knowing it's time for me to let go of the night and move on, I still only feel good things about it.

I only feel ashamed I want more.

I stare down at my knees as the wind picks up and roars around the house with a renewed fury that raises goosebumps on my arms. Caleb hugs Greta harder, mumbles something about hoping Clementine is okay in the barn. Ben is the picture of stillness, sitting with crossed legs and a straight back, his eyes on the weather radio as it drones on and on about tornado sightings near Holm and which counties need to take cover.

There's something about Ben's stillness that betrays *something*, however, even if I can't put my finger on it. It's not the stillness of a person at peace but the stillness of a person who's trained themselves not to flinch, and it makes me wonder what else Ben has trained himself to do.

And why.

A huge clatter comes from upstairs, followed by a glass-shattering crash, and Caleb jolts, as if to get up, but Ben clamps a hand on his shoulder. "Stay the fuck here," Ben bites out.

Caleb looks up the stairs, torn, and I remember he told me on our tour around the place that this is his family's house, that it's over a hundred years old. No wonder he feels protective.

But Ben is right—whatever is happening above us is too dangerous to investigate, and I watch his hand on Caleb's shoulder for longer than I should, something about it making me hot and squirmy all over again.

The weather radio keeps droning, but the wind and crashing get louder and louder, drowning out the robotic voice coming through the small, old speakers, and there's a moment when I think the house is going to come right off the foundations and just blow away. It rattles and creaks and groans mightily, and I realize I've grabbed on to Caleb's thigh only after he takes my hand and rubs a soothing thumb over the back of it.

The house seems besieged for hours, but when the weather radio announces the time, it's only been a handful of minutes, and from there on out, the wind slowly abates, retreating with erratic and fitful gusts, until all is silent once more. The next time the weather radio lists the counties that need to take cover, our county isn't on the list.

Ben clicks it off.

"Ready?" he asks us, as if we're about to go into battle and not upstairs. Neither Caleb nor I answer, although I notice Caleb gives Greta an extra pat before shifting her off his lap, and I think it's more to comfort him than to reassure her.

After blowing out the candles, we mount the creaking stairs up to the ground floor, with Ben's bobbing flashlight to guide us, and then he swings the door open to reveal a house that's still intact.

"Oh, thank fuck," Caleb breathes as we walk around to see everything is where it should be. The screen door came loose in the wind, apparently, and banged against the side of the house hard enough to shatter the glass in the lower half of it, but the rest of the windows are intact, and when we walk around the outside, the siding and the roof seem to be fine. Even Clementine is okay when we check on her, although she's agitated. The worst thing we can find is a tree on the edge of the property that's been blown over and some sunflower petals scattered across the lawn.

Caleb visibly brightens the more we walk, and he's nearly smiling when we get back to the house. Even Greta is wagging her tail, and for a moment, I think it's all over—the storm, the fear, the worry—all of it.

Then Ben's phone rings.

CHAPTER TEN

BEN

I don't like storms. Never have, actually, but after I got back from my last deployment, I realized I *really* don't like them. Not the unpredictable rolls of thunder that remind me of mortars echoing through lonely, scree-covered valleys. Not the strobes of lightning that remind me of muzzle flashes at a distance. But weirdly, it is the wind that gets me the most. My therapist says it's because the wind is as unpredictable as the thunder, but I know it's more than that.

The thing is, wind can sound like anything it wants—a screaming man, the whirr of helicopter blades, trucks rolling over the dirt. Any sound, every sound. One minute I'm in my own bed, and the next I'm back there. Kabul. Marjah and Musa Qala in the Helmand Province. The godforsaken Korengal. All I wanted was to come home. And then I came home and it was like it didn't matter.

But last night, I came the closest I have in years to falling asleep during a storm, to falling asleep in the same bed as someone else. Maybe it was the very thorough fuck session, but maybe it was also Ireland herself. Watching me with parted lips and openly curious eyes while a contented and happy Caleb snored behind her.

It's been so long since anyone has looked at me like that, like they genuinely wanted to know what was howling inside me, like they wouldn't be scared of it if I let it out. Like they wouldn't be upset if they cracked me open and actually found *nothing* inside, howling or not.

If they found there is no *Ben* inside me any longer, that I've somehow become a shell, a puppet pretending to be Ben Weber, going through the motions as if he never decided ROTC would be a handy way to pay for college. As if he just decided to stay near Holm and work at a bar and fuck women and his best friend at the same time.

Caleb's the only person I'll ever trust with the mess I've become, precisely because he doesn't demand to see those messy truths if I'm not willing to show them. But Ireland... Her gaze last night both demanded and conceded, and it evoked something fiercely needy in me, something that wanted to tie her to Caleb's bed and have her look at me that way forever. It was so unnerving that I had to leave after she fell asleep, although I would have left anyway. I'm too vulnerable in the nighttime.

I prefer to be vulnerable in private.

What is it about Ireland that makes me think I could change that? Even today, I find myself drawn to her clear blue gaze and her voice, which has the slightly husky sound of a woman who's just woken up. I want to fuck her right here in the branch-strewn yard right after a fucking tornado, that's how sexy her voice is.

In fact, I'm listening to her talk when my phone rings,

jarring and loud compared to the low, sultry music of Ireland's words. With a muttered curse, I step away and answer it. It's Debbie, one of my two employees at the tavern.

"Ben," she says, and there's a peculiar and specific tremble in her voice that I've heard a hundred times before but never from her.

Never here at home.

Shock.

She's in shock.

I close my eyes, for a minute both smelling and tasting gunpowder. Feeling grit and dirt under my eyelids and on my lips.

"What is it?" I manage.

"The tavern," she shakes out. "Ben, the whole town, it's just—"

I understand immediately, even though I don't want to. I thought we'd been spared the worst of the storm; I thought we'd been lucky.

Turns out the worst of it didn't hit the farm because it was too busy tearing apart the town. The place I grew up, the place I earn my living. The place I call home.

"Are you safe?" I ask first because it's the most important thing. "Is everyone safe?"

"I don't know," she says. "I only just got here from my place. There's a police car, but I—I don't know. I don't know."

Shock will do that. Make the simplest sentences break off into fragments, make even the easy thoughts impossible to hold on to. I know exactly how Debbie feels right now because I've felt it so many times before. Although never *here*, never where I thought I was safe, with the wide green fields and leafy trees and sleepy creeks.

I squeeze my hand into a fist so tight I feel the nails dig into my palm.

"I'll be right there," I tell her.

♦ ♦ ♦ ♦

Caleb didn't need to hear anything from me when I hung up the phone. Somehow he had shirts for us. Somehow he herded me toward his truck, and Ireland and Greta ended up between us on the big bench seat. Somehow we made it the two miles to Holm without saying a single word to each other.

And then we roll to the edge of our small town, and I'm beyond words anyway. I'm too busy remembering the sound of boots scrabbling over dusty ground, the heavy spray of gunfire in the heat. The scene we come upon is a scene I thought I'd never have to see again, a scene I saw far the fuck too often: the mounded rubble of a town gashed right off the map.

Holm is gone.

Well, maybe not *gone* entirely, but close to it—close enough that it's unrecognizable as the place I've called home for thirty-four years, and close enough that I almost wish it *were* entirely gone, because now it's become something tragic and alien and chaotic beyond belief.

The big trees shading Main Street are snapped and whittled to sharp, stark masts of stripped lumber, and the green lampposts that used to light the street—the ones the American Legion and Auxiliary Club decorate for Christmas each year—are knocked over like Lincoln Logs. Trash and debris litter every available surface—shreds of fluffy, pink insulation from the mowed-over homes a block away, glass and lumber snapped into toothpicks, paper and jagged slabs of sheetrock, and drifts of shingles and bricks piled as high as banks of snow.

"Fuck," Caleb says, stunned. "*Fuck*."

I don't say anything but climb out of the truck and walk toward the bar. I hear Ireland and Greta follow me, but I don't turn back to look at them. I don't trust myself; I don't trust that Ireland won't give me one of those clear, demanding looks, and I'll crack into a thousand pieces right here in the middle of all this ruin. I can't crack, not yet. Not before I make sure everyone is safe and I know what all needs to be done.

Holm is small—less than four hundred people, and even that number has probably shrunk some since the last census—and our Main Street is only four blocks long. My bar is at the end of it, in an old brick building that's been around since the town's founding. It used to be the general store before they opened a Walmart off the interstate exchange, and the old salt who opened the bar in the 1980s called it General's to honor the building's past. I kept the name when I bought the place, and it's a strange relief to see it in faded paint still on the side of the building.

But everything else about the bar is wrong.

The windows are blown out. The door is gone. The brick structure survived, but the bricks themselves are blasted and chipped all to shit. And the inside looks like a ruin of glass, furniture, and ceiling tiles.

I crunch my way inside, squinting up into the shadows to make sure the ceiling isn't about to fall on my head, and call out, "Hello?" There's nothing but the sound of dripping water and voices from outside.

I step back out onto the street, looking for any sign of police or paramedics, wondering if the bar has been searched for people—and the other buildings on Main Street and houses too. It's been about thirty minutes since we left the basement on the farm. Surely that's enough time for first responders to arrive?

Caleb joins me after a minute, trailed by a shell-shocked Ireland and a nervous Greta. "Just talked to Harley from the gas station," he says. "They've been through all the buildings on this side."

"They find anyone?"

Caleb looks down the street in that *My Antonia* way of his, all stoic and solemn while the prairie wind tugs gently at his shirt and hair. "Three bodies. They've laid them out in the park, near the water tower. Called a funeral home over in Emporia already." Caleb names who they found, two of whom were Sunday school teachers of mine and one of whom we went to high school with, and I stagger—actually stagger—against the now-bruised wall of my bar. I lean my head back against the brick, close my eyes, and try to breathe, try to remain present, try all the tricks my therapist has given me, but it's no good. I feel jagged and angry and emptier than ever. I feel like the building I'm leaning against, like something that's been broken and tossed away and left to crumble in its own desperate mess.

And that's when Ireland steps past me to walk inside the bar. I open my eyes to see her curvy frame disappear into the gloom, and for a single, shining second, I recognize everything is going to be okay. That there might be a future with this sexy woman and her penetrating gaze and her secret bravery.

I take in a deep breath.

And then the ceiling falls in on top of her.

CHAPTER ELEVEN

IRELAND

"I'm fine!" I shout. "I'm fine! I'm fine!"

Okay, maybe *fine* is a little bit of a lie, given there's God only knows how many pounds of wood and metal pipe making a very unsteady tent above my head, but I'm not dead and I don't think I'm injured, at least not seriously so. Something hit my shoulder fairly hard on the way down, and I think I'll have an almighty scrape on my leg, but nothing's broken and nothing's bleeding in any alarming kind of way. Mostly I'm just covered in sheetrock dust.

"Jesus Christ," I hear Caleb swear viciously, and I see something in front of me shift, letting a little bit more light into the unsteady tent of mine. "You're really okay?"

"Help me," Ben's voice comes through. "Move that there—not that beam; it'll send everything else crashing down. Yes, there, that one. One, two, *three*—"

Ben's voice is knowledgeable, authoritative. Despite everything—the pain and the ruin around us and the very real danger I'm in of this stuff falling on me—I shiver a little at the reminder of how commanding he can be. How he commanded Caleb and me last night.

And in less than ten minutes, they've got the remains of the ceiling moved enough for me to wriggle free. There's an awkward moment where I don't quite fit and they have to shift more pieces around, and I have the sudden, familiar rush of longing for a different body—which is patently ridiculous, as *this* body was nearly just crushed by a building and I should only feel gratitude for being alive, so I shove that longing where it belongs and work my way free of the debris pile.

The minute I have my torso mostly out, I'm abruptly yanked into two sets of strong arms and crushed between two chests.

"I thought you were dead," Ben says roughly. I can barely breathe for how tightly I'm held between them, and I feel lips—his and Caleb's—all over my hair, and I feel their hearts drumming against my body in a frantic tattoo.

This is not how you treat someone you never see again.

Maybe they want to keep me.

But within seconds, Ben tramples the fledgling hope inside me. He pulls away from me so fast I almost stumble forward. And when I see his face, it's not even the cold expression I've grown used to from him. It's something wild and furious.

"You should go," he harshes out. "Go home."

Stupid me, I think *home* means the farm, and I say, "I'm not going home until you two are."

He shakes his head, almost violently, sending his too-long hair flicking into his face. "Go to *your* home, Ireland," he says, his eyes turbulent with something I don't understand. "You can't be here anymore!"

Oh.

Oh.

My heart sinks, even as I cling to any reason I can stay. "I still have work to do here," I protest faintly. "Pictures to take."

Ben makes a dangerous noise. "Look around you, sweetheart. You think this is the kind of picture your boss wants?"

I glance around the storm-wrecked bar and outside the door to Main Street, which looks just as broken, just as bad.

Caleb lets go of me, although I can feel the reluctance in him, and that gives me the courage to try one last time.

"I could stay...?" I offer. "And help?"

There's that cold curl to Ben's mouth now, something almost like a sneer, and I wonder how can this be the man who just crushed me against his chest, the man who just frantically kissed my hair as if to reassure himself I was alive? How?

How can he just *change*? Close off like this?

"Just get out of here, Ireland," Ben says, and his entire body is tensed with something that's either panic or fury. "Don't make this awkward."

And those are the words.

Those are the words that slap me across the face—more than *go home*, more than *it's time for you to leave*.

Don't make this awkward.

Don't be *that* fat girl. Don't be the girl so desperate for affection that she abandons all pretense of dignity and begs for it. Don't be eager, and don't be clingy.

Don't draw attention to yourself.

Don't ask for more than what people want to give you, because they won't want to give you much.

I know these *don't*s. They've been my rulebook since high school, my guiding principles, and every decision I've made since turning down that photography scholarship has been because of the *don't*s. How could I have fooled myself into thinking last night was something special? I know better—*I know better*—and I still let myself hope the adventure could last.

"Ireland," Caleb says, something pained in his voice. But I'm already turning away, I'm already leaving. Crunching over the bricks and glass outside to...to where, exactly?

To the farm, I decide. I'll walk to the farm. It's only a couple of miles, and there are only two turns. I can find my way, get my things. Then I'll walk to my car and leave for home.

They want me to go? Fine. I know the *don't*s inside and out. I have them tattooed on the beating flesh of my heart. I know them even better than they do.

I won't make anything awkward.

I'll go.

♦ ♦ ♦ ♦

"Ireland, wait!" Caleb calls, jogging up next to me. I'm already to the edge of town, past the place where he'd parked his truck. I'm guessing he stayed behind to talk to Ben, and I'm also guessing that whatever that conversation consisted of would piss me off, so I'm not going to ask about it. Instead, I turn and say, "Yes?" like he's a complete stranger to me.

Hurt flickers through those green eyes, and for a moment, I feel bad. Then I remember Ben's cruel words, and I regret nothing.

"Please, Ireland, I—" He squints down at the ground and scratches at his head, as if he's so lost for words he can't even remember how to speak them aloud. "I'm—I'm sorry, I guess. I mean, I don't *guess* that I'm sorry, I know I am, but sorry isn't all I want to say. I just don't know how to say the rest."

Just go. Just keep walking.

But it's like I unbottled part of myself last night, and I can't remember how to bottle it again. "*Sorry* isn't an even exchange for being treated like that," I say, hoping my voice flays him open. Hoping each word is a penknife under his fingernails. And he does flinch and opens his mouth to say something, but I stop him. "If you and Ben don't want to fuck me again, that's fine, but I don't deserve to be shooed away like a dog."

Caleb slumps his broad shoulders at this. "You're right. Of course not."

I start walking again, and he follows me.

I sigh and stop again. "Is this your way of offering me a ride to the farm?" I ask. And even as I ask it, there's a part of me that hopes he'll say no, that he's coming after me to tell me to stay, to tell me that Ben didn't mean it.

To tell me they both want me to stay.

But he doesn't tell me that.

"Yes," he replies. "I'm not letting you walk all the way back to the farm. Or to your car. And I've already talked to them on the phone, but I'd like to check on Mrs. Parry and Mrs. Harthcock, so I'm headed that direction anyway."

Ah, how gentlemanly, I think bitterly. A real gentleman should always give last night's trollop a ride back to her car, especially if it's on his way to do other things.

Caleb trots off to fetch his truck, and within a few minutes, I'm inside the cab as the ancient air conditioning roars hot air in our faces and as I try to wipe as much of the sheetrock dust off my face as I can. My hair is a lost cause—I look like I took a shower with grit instead of water—but I still pick out the bigger pieces of gypsum and flick them out the window. I'm examining the scrape on my thigh as we pull onto the gravel driveway of the farm.

Caleb parks the truck and then looks over at me for a minute.

"Get on the porch," he says gruffly. "I'll get something for that scrape."

"I don't need—"

He cuts me a glance that brooks no argument. "On the porch, Ireland. Before I haul you there myself." And then he slides out of the truck and slams the door behind him, stalking toward the house.

Sitting on the hot vinyl seat for a moment longer, I consider my options...and then decide it would be stupid to refuse a bandage just because my feelings are hurt. I'll get the scrape taken care of, and then I'll get my things, and then I'll go. Back to my empty apartment and my stable, safe job and my fridge full of whatever new diet shake my sister wants me to try.

And maybe I'm going to take a break from adventures.

Turns out they hurt a lot when they end.

I finally get out of the truck and sit on one of the old chairs clustered into a corner of the porch. Caleb emerges from the house with a first aid kit in hand. He drops to his knees in front of me, and he's so tall that even when he kneels, he's eye-level with me in the chair.

He clicks open the kit, reaches for my leg, and then hesitates. "May I?" he asks.

"Sure," I say. Grumpily.

The scrape starts near the outside of my knee and angles inward to the sensitive skin of my inner thigh. Caleb gently parts my legs in order to reach it, and my entire body lights up like a Christmas tree.

I suck in a breath.

So does he.

There's no denying the charge between us, despite what just happened, despite the fact that I'm going to leave. Despite the fact that he and Ben *want* me to leave.

No, feeling the warm brush of his torso and arms as he settles between my legs still affects me. Still makes my belly tighten low around the lingering soreness he left inside me last night.

And I can tell he feels it too. His hands shake the slightest bit as he grabs the antiseptic spray and a gauze pad, and when he looks back up at me before he sprays the scrape, I can see his pulse hammering in his neck.

"This may sting," he whispers.

"It can't hurt more than anything else that's happened today," I tell him, initially meaning the ceiling collapse but then realizing he may think I mean Ben's ugly words instead.

Well. Maybe I do.

His eyes look sad, and there's no trace of that amazing dimple under his beard. With an acknowledging nod, he bends low over my leg and sprays the scrape.

"Ouch!" I hiss, but my hiss turns into a moan as he leans close to my thigh and blows over the parts that sting. "Oh. *Oh.* Caleb."

He shudders at the sound of his name on my lips, blowing a little harder and then kissing all around the scrape, careful not to touch it, not to hurt me more. And then his mouth is moving up and up and up, right to the hem of my shorts, with licks and nibbles that have me squirming.

"Let me taste you," he begs. "Please. Let me taste you again."

And all of my hurt irritation vanishes in a puff of pure lust at the thought of Caleb's mouth on my pussy, at the promise of even more beard-burn, and suddenly I'm wriggling out of my shorts, half standing, half hopping, reaching over to the porch railing for balance.

I manage to kick them off, but before I can sit back down, I'm pushed against the railing and my panties are yanked to the side, and then Caleb's hot mouth is on me, sowing sweet fire everywhere he touches.

"God, you're already so wet," he mumbles against me, giving my pussy another openmouthed kiss, followed by a long lick with the flat of his tongue. "Always so wet for us."

Us.

Ben's absence is like a hole in the air, sucking all the oxygen away from us, and I hate that I want him here even after he kicked me to the curb. I hate that I miss his touch on me so much it hurts.

I hate it.

Even as I can't deny it.

"Fuck, you taste good," Caleb murmurs. His strong fingers dig into the soft rounds of my ass, keeping my pussy angled the way he likes, and the feeling of those almost-bruising fingertips along with the chafe of his beard drives me perilously close to orgasm. His tongue seems to be everywhere, until he gently takes my clit between his teeth and suckles at it.

My head falls back as I give a long moan. "God, Caleb, oh my God."

But I don't keep my head back, because he's too delicious right now, and I never want to forget how he looks like this. On his knees in front of me, those big shoulders tucked in, his dark head below the curve of my still-clothed stomach, tilting and working...

It's so much to feel, so much to see, even as awful questions filter through my mind.

Are you doing this out of pity?

Why doesn't Ben want me?

How am I supposed to walk away from this?

But even the questions disappear into smoky nothing as my impending orgasm winds closer and closer and closer, and I arch against the railing, trying to push myself harder against Caleb's wicked tongue.

He responds with a hungry, eager groan, sucking and licking like his life depends on it, and then I'm done for. I pant out his name right as my climax bursts, and then I don't know what else I'm saying. Curses, blessings, maybe even Ben's name leaves my mouth, but it doesn't matter, because it feels so fucking good. Waves and waves starting in my clit and radiating out through my stomach and thighs and all the way to the tips of my fingers. It feels like it goes on for hours as I ride it out against his mouth, with one hand braced on the railing and the other hand in his hair, clutching him tight.

And then, gradually, as all good things do, it subsides. It goes away, leaving only weak knees and a full-body flush in its wake.

Caleb seems reluctant to stop eating me, but he does, tilting his head up with half-lidded eyes and wet lips. He looks intoxicated—intoxicated from *me*, my body—which is a heady feeling. Heady as fuck. And when I look all the way down his body, I know for certain pity had nothing to do with what just happened.

He's hard.

Hard enough to seriously tent his jeans.

For a moment, we linger like this, my hand still twined in his hair and him on his knees with his face canted up toward mine, like a sinner before God. His eyes blaze earnestly across my face, and my stomach twists as I recognize what he's doing.

He's committing me to memory.

I let go of his hair.

"Ireland," he says as I bend over to grab my shorts. "Please."

I don't know what to make of him, this honest, passionate man who can make honest, passionate love to me and still say goodbye afterward. I don't know what to make of Ben either, and the thought that I'll never have the opportunity to figure them out is sharp enough to make me pull my shorts on with haste. I need to leave. Before I do something truly awkward, like cry.

Caleb stands, licking his lips like he's licking the last of my taste off them, and renewed lust hits me low below the belly button. I ignore it and fasten my shorts.

"I'll just go get my things," I announce, pointlessly, and he follows me into the house and up the stairs like a puppy. A big farmer puppy with big farmer muscles and pleading green eyes.

Ugh. Why do the two of them have to be so unfairly handsome? What chance do I stand against that?

I go into the guest room and pull together my things to pack, and from behind me, Caleb says, "Ben was in the army."

"Okay," I say, keeping my back to him as I fold up my clothes and stuff them into my bag. "Thanks for telling me."

"No, I—" Caleb makes that frustrated noise that tells me he's frustrated with himself, with the way he can't explain things the way he wants. "Ben was in Afghanistan. Four tours."

That slows me down. I put my camera on the bed next to my bag and turn to face him. "Okay," I say again, but curiously this time. I'm listening. Thinking of the way Ben kept so still this morning to avoid flinching at the *booms* of the thunder. Why he has trouble sleeping.

"I think it was bad. I mean, I know it was bad. He was in so many of the places you'd see on the news, and he knew so many people who died or were seriously injured, and I think he saw a lot of fucked-up things. He was always so sensitive..."

I make a noise at that, thinking of his cold eyes, his sneering smiles. "Ben? Sensitive?"

Caleb sighs. "Yeah. He used to get bullied a lot, as a kid, before he filled out in high school."

"God. Why?"

Caleb shrugs. "Because kids are awful? Because his sister was older than him and already out? Because he could never hide how he felt about anything?"

I ask the obvious question. "Were you two in love as kids?"

He rubs the back of his neck. "No...and yes. We've always been close. He lived with his grandma growing up, and after she had to move to a home, my parents unofficially took him in. His sister had already gone off to college at that point, but she wasn't ready to be responsible for another person, I guess."

"So you lived together? Is that when you found out you wanted each other?"

"It was complicated, you know? It didn't—I don't think either of us knew until the first time we had a third person. Someone between us."

"When was that?" I sit on the bed now, reluctantly enthralled. "High school?"

"A cheerleader named Serena." A faint smile blooms on Caleb's face. "She had a crush on both of us, and we both liked her. For a while, I thought we were going to fight for her, but then we all got drunk at a field party and the three of us ended up together in the back of my truck. We did that a few more times, until she started dating a basketball player instead."

"And you never..." I wave with my hand to indicate what I mean. "Never just the two of you?"

"We did," Caleb admits softly. His ears go red, but he meets my eyes so I'll know he's being completely honest. "Just the two of us. The summer after graduation."

"And?"

"It was still *fun*," he replies, with an almost shy smile, as if even the word *fun* is impossibly dirty, "but there was something about being a three that fit us better than being a two."

I think about that for a moment. Think about how electric it felt last night to be between the two of them, because it *was* electric and somehow also comforting—like nothing I've ever felt before in bed. As if between the three of us we could handle anything, we could explore everywhere, our shared strength and energy creating a web of safety and affection all around us.

I look out the window at the barn, where the three of us fooled around last night, wondering if maybe I fit better in a three than a two myself. Or is it just Caleb and Ben? Even if I left here and found another set of boys to play with, would it be the same?

I sigh. *How could it be the same? When it's* them *I want so much, not the number?*

"So we went to college and dated around for a while," Caleb continues. "And it was at the end of freshman year that my dad took me aside to have a chat. Turns out our little college flings had made their way through the town gossips back to him."

I grimace, and Caleb just laughs.

"Don't worry, he didn't kill me. Instead, he told me about Mrs. Parry's sister."

"What about her?" I ask, a little confused.

"She lived with two men on the other side of Holm for fifty years."

"Oh," I respond in a surprised voice. "That's unusual."

"The more unusual part is that I guess the town got used

to it. She and her two men were part of everything—church, Rotary club, town picnics. And my dad told me if Ben and I wanted to live that way, the town would accept us. And he said if we wanted to be a couple, just the two of us, then he'd make sure the town accepted us that way too."

"And did they?" I ask. "Accept you?"

"Yeah," Caleb says with a smile. "They did. Mackenna lived with us for four years after college, and we never had to hide it. Not here in Holm, at least. People stared a bit in the beginning, when the three of us would hold hands or share a blanket during the town parade, but they got used to it fast. Maybe even bored with it. And after she left, when it was just the two of us together, it was the same way."

"Huh." It goes against everything I've ever thought about small towns, being a city girl myself, but maybe there's something about a tightly knit community that can absorb differences in surprising ways. "When did Mackenna leave? *Why* did she leave?"

Caleb's smile drops and drops fast. He looks out the window and rubs the back of his neck again. "She left nearly five years ago. Honest, it doesn't keep me up at night, but for Ben—well, Ben's the reason she left."

"Why? Was he a jerk to her too?" I ask a little bitterly.

"No," Caleb says simply. "He just...*wasn't.* Wasn't anything. When we met her in college, Ben was still that sensitive boy, but after each tour, it was like less and less of him came back. When he came back home the final time, he was sealed off so tight he could barely breathe. Mackenna always was an impatient kind of person, and it only took a few months of trying to bring him back before she gave up. She moved to the city, and that was that."

Even though he was a dick earlier, my heart still twists a little for Ben, the sensitive boy who went to war and came back a shell. "Has Ben...you know. Seen anyone? About what happened to him?"

"He's been going to a therapist weekly for five years now," Caleb says, a touch of pride in his voice. "He sees a psychiatrist too—meds for his panic attacks and sleeping problems—and he's in a community support group with other veterans. He's been working on himself for years, Ireland, so he hasn't just been lying around broken waiting for someone to fix him."

"I never said he was," I shoot back, ruffled. "Just that today he seemed awfully sealed off. And a lot like an asshole."

I watch as a certain kind of defeat scrawls itself across Caleb's face. "I know. I think—I think seeing the town gutted like that brought back some hard memories. And I think when that ceiling fell on you—well, fuck, Ireland, even I thought you were dead for a moment, and it hurt like nothing I've ever felt before."

I want to cling to the *maybes* his words raise in my mind—I want to cling to them too much, I can already feel it. Just like I can feel the tears burning at my eyelids when I ask, "If that's true, then how can *you* say goodbye?"

He rubs at his beard, his jaw tight and his eyes shining. "Because we start things together, and we finish them together. I'm sorry, Ireland, I really am, but that's the way it has to be."

♦ ♦ ♦ ♦

Fifteen minutes later, I'm in my Prius, bumping toward the interstate. In my rearview, I still see Caleb's truck and him standing outside it. He refuses to leave until he sees me safely on my way. I know that's what he's doing, and it's the final straw.

I finally let the tears flow now. Now, when it won't be *awkward*. Now, when I can save my pride.

Everywhere there are signs of the storm and the destruction it scattered around the countryside. Branches down, big green road signs crumpled as if by a giant fist. Leaves and twigs everywhere, along with a scattering of things that are far, far from their homes. An Easy Bake oven lodged in a tree. A mattress blown against a fence.

And yet nothing the storm has left even comes close to matching how messy and broken I feel right now.

I think I fell in love. I think I fell in love in a single night. I think I fell in love with two people instead of one, and all of it is ridiculous, so fucking ridiculous, but that doesn't stop it from being true.

Doesn't stop it one bit.

Soon, Caleb's truck is out of sight, and I'm turning onto the paved county road that will take me back to the highway. Across the junction is a grassy field, but through the plot of knee-high grass waving in the sunny breeze is a meandering swath of flattened stalks, bent and speckled with flung mud. It's a near perfect depiction of the path of the tornado, and there's something singularly striking about it.

Possibly the lonely destruction matches my mood.

I reach automatically for my camera in the bag on the passenger seat, shoving my hand through my clothes in search of its reassuring shape, its familiar heft. But even as I riffle through the bag, a vision suddenly comes to me of my camera on the bed in the farmhouse's guest room. I put it there while Caleb was telling me about Ben and him, and I got so caught up in the story that I completely forgot to shove it into the bag before I left.

Which means it's still at the farmhouse.

Fuck.

I pointlessly and stupidly smack the steering wheel with my palm, which only hurts my hand and makes me feel childish. And childish is not something I can afford to feel right now—not when I'm already the awkward sausage who couldn't take a hint and had to be told to leave.

Humiliation and anger burn at me as I yank on the wheel of the car to make a vicious U-turn back to the farm. The humiliation is for obvious reasons, I suppose, but even I don't entirely understand the anger. I'm not an angry person normally; in fact, I'm always the first to say sorry, the first to make peace. I usually do everything I can to avoid conflict, to keep people liking me.

You're done with that now. No more apologizing just because you're scared of people walking away.

I straighten in my seat as I drive back to the farmhouse, and I allow the anger to wash away the humiliation. I allow myself, for the first time in my life, to hang on to my anger, to feed it and embrace it. Even with Brian and my sister, I never gave myself permission to be angry. Escaping those relationships were acts of desperate survival and retreat, not blazing righteousness. But it's like the storm—and what happened in Caleb's bed as it raged around us—has finally unlocked some new store of pride I've never had before.

I'm furious that these men made me feel any doubt or embarrassment about the night we spent together. I'm furious that the way Ben treated me made me feel like a stereotype. I'm furious that the whole thing made me feel ugly and unlovable.

And mostly, I'm furious that I live in a world that has the power to make me feel ugly and unlovable because of my body.

I'm very aware that Ben is still scowling and prowling his way around his wrecked business, that Caleb is off playing Farmer Do-Gooder, and that the farmhouse will be empty. All the same, I find myself rehearsing triumphant speeches and searing retorts all the way back to the Carpenter farm. For the first time in my life, I feel emboldened to defend my body. I feel proud of it, and I almost *want* someone to be at the house so I can tell them exactly how I feel. So I can hear my words scorching the air as I stand in my own skin and assert my right to be treated with dignity and to be loved. My right to live as everyone else lives.

In fucking peace.

Since the storm broke up this morning, the sun has been baking down on the prairie, and even the gloppy mud of the road has hardened enough for the Prius to wobble over it without issue. It wobbles back to the farm, and as I pull into the driveway, I see with a surge of excitement, dismay—and yes, lust—that it seems like I'll be getting my wish.

Ben is here.

CHAPTER TWELVE

BEN

I know it the moment it happens. Telling Ireland to go is the biggest mistake of my life.

I know it like I know the Kansas sun on my back or the weight of body armor on my shoulders. I know it like I know the green of Caleb's eyes.

I know it so much it hurts.

But even as I watched her wheel around to leave—gorgeous even covered in dust—I still couldn't make myself go after her. She almost *died* because of me, and how many people were hurt and killed right in front of me in rubble-strewn hellholes just like this one? It's sheer luck she's alive, and the knives of terror that stabbed through me while we were digging her out drove so deep I couldn't think straight.

Then the soldier in me took over, because that's what happens when I panic now. The sensitive boy who would have cowered behind Caleb at the first sign of trouble—he had no one to cower behind in Afghanistan. And so he learned to survive on his own.

I don't even really know what all I said to Ireland to make her leave—only that I followed her flinches to the words that would hurt the most, the ones that would drive her away. Words that would condemn me to hell, but even as I held her in my arms frantically kissing her hair, my brain wouldn't stop shouting *get her to safety, keep her safe, keep her safe, get her out*—

It was the only thing that penetrated the lingering terror and the relief she was okay—relief so deep that I knew I was already falling in love with her.

Keep her safe.

Keep her from harm.

Get her out.

"What the fuck?" Caleb demands. He's scrubbing at his face like he does when he's frustrated. When he's furious. "Why the *fuck* would you say something like that?"

My mind is still looping through its carousel of nightmares—the ceiling coming down over Ireland, blood-spattered dust in Helmand, yanking on debris not knowing if I'll find a corpse underneath—and I can't force out the right words. "She needed to leave," I say instead, my voice harsh and shaking. "She needed to go."

"No, asshole, she didn't," Caleb spits out. "I thought you liked her. I thought you understood that *I* liked her. That I wanted more than just a night with her."

I can't reply because I *do* like her. I *do* understand. I also want more with her, lots and lots and lots more, but my head is still crowded with flashes of her trapped under the wreckage and old memories from the war, and my heart is still squeezing with panic and the desperate need to get her to someplace safe, someplace *away*.

"Goddammit, Ben, answer me," Caleb grates out. "Just fucking answer me. You don't get to be a shell, not right fucking now. You don't get to go cold and empty after what you just did."

A shell. Cold and empty.

I hear the words like a faraway train, knowing what they are, yet they're so distant I can't reach them.

"She had to go someplace away from here," is all I can manage, and Caleb's jaw sets. He's so fucking handsome like this, streaked with dust, his beard setting off the perfect planes of his face. He's so handsome...but he's looking at me now with an expression of pure disgust.

"We've always done things together, Ben, and I won't stop now. But I also don't know if she'll ever forgive you for this, and I don't know if I ever will either."

And with that, my best friend, lover, and essential part of any relationship I've ever had, walks out the door.

♦ ♦ ♦ ♦

It takes me almost an hour.

I'm behind the bar, sitting with my head between my knees the way I used to sit after getting roughed up by bullies in school, and I'm trying to do all the breathing exercises they teach you in therapy. I'm trying to put all the bad memories back where they belong and pull myself back to the present.

It's hard.

It's harder than it's been in years. It takes all the things I've learned plus the sedate presence of Greta-dog curled up next to me to claw my way up and out.

At some point, I slowly surface again. I can think Real-Ben thoughts and not Shell-Ben thoughts. I realize with dawning horror what I've done. I've hurt Ireland. In my mindless need to stop the terror, I've hurt her, and it gouges a fresh hole in my scarred heart.

I stumble out of the bar, my heart hammering against my ribs and anxiety crawling up the back of my neck, and there's no sign of Ireland or Caleb anywhere. Even Caleb's truck is gone.

He took her back to the farmhouse. Maybe they're still there?

God, let them still be there.

I bolt down the sidewalk, Greta at my heels, both of us dodging debris and the haggard townspeople milling around the ruined Main Street. It's a testament to how awful the day is that no one seems to notice or care that the town barkeep and his dog are sprinting back home, not that I'd care if anyone did notice.

My mind is full of Ireland and her blue eyes brimming with wounded hurt. Of Caleb and his disappointment.

I have to get to the farm. *Now.* Because I can't bear to lose Ireland, and if I do lose Ireland, I may also lose Caleb, and I also can't bear that. I won't survive losing either of them.

I'd rather go back to war.

The two miles home are hot and punishing, but if there's one thing I carried over from the army, it's the habit of going on hot and punishing runs, so I make decent time, even though I arrive a sweaty mess and Greta arrives soaked after taking her detours through farm ponds and stock tanks along the way.

It doesn't matter what time I make, though. No one's here.

I walk through the house in a numb kind of daze, set out cool water for Greta, and then wander upstairs. I don't bother calling any names—the emptiness in the house is palpable, almost like a living thing itself.

I go to the guestroom where Ireland would have stayed and stand at the foot of the bed, my hands dangling uselessly at my sides. I just stare in a kind of blank hurt at it. I know I don't deserve this moment of pain, so close to self-pity, because every part of this is my fault, but I'm also not strong enough to push the hurt away. I indulge in it and let it take me because I deserve to hurt. I deserve this shame and loneliness.

Sweat from my run here burns my eyes, and I wipe roughly at my face with an equally sweaty arm, which only makes it worse. With a sharp growl of frustration, I yank the unused guest towel that Ireland left folded neatly on the still-neatly made bed—neatly made because she slept with *us* last night—to dry my face.

That's when it catches my eye. Her camera, sleek and expensive, still nestled atop the faded quilt.

She wouldn't have left that on purpose.

Maybe she'll come back for it.

My heart lifts at the thought and then crashes back down, because even if she comes back for it, even if I get to see her pretty heart-shaped face and luscious body again, it doesn't mean I have a right to ask for more.

Like asking her to listen. Asking her to stay.

Making up for my earlier cruelty with as much pleasure as I can possibly visit on her body.

But still I find myself taking the camera in my hand, thinking about how her hands must have cradled it in exactly the same way.

It makes me feel closer to her.

I stopped questioning myself and my feelings when it comes to sex and love a long time ago—the way Caleb and I love each other necessitates a certain amount of adaptability and spontaneity—but I still can't help wondering about my feelings. To be so gone for someone after only a night? It's never happened to me before—not with Mackenna and not even with Caleb. Both of those relationships gradually evolved over time. But falling for Ireland was like an explosion—jagged and fiery and quick as hell.

By the time I heard the *click*, it'd already gone *boom*.

I go out on the porch, as if that will somehow bring her back to me. I'm clutching her camera like a child clutches a toy when I see the distinctive glint of sunlight on metal coming from the north.

My chest tightens; something inside it flips over and flips over hard.

Ireland.

The length of another breath brings a little Prius into view, bright blue and flecked with mud, and I know for sure it's her. I know that somehow I'm being given another chance, and I decide I'm taking it no matter fucking what. I'll beg her to listen, and I'll never stop begging if that's what it takes. I fucked up, but I'll spend the rest of my life making it up to her, if only she'll let me.

Oh God, please. Please let me, sweetheart.

♦ ♦ ♦ ♦

"I'm just here for my camera," she announces briskly as she climbs out of her car. She's still in her distractingly sexy shorts and clingy tank top from earlier, and there's still sheetrock dust in her hair, but she has a bandage on her leg now and a heat in her eyes that means she's either furious or aroused. Or both.

Hot blood kicks to my groin, and I feel myself thicken against my zipper. Fuck, I want her. Even furious with me, I want her. I want her to scratch at me as she holds my face to her pussy. I want her to bite my neck and shoulder and chest as her heels dig into my back to drive me deeper inside her.

I hand over her camera without any additional urging from her. I'm not interested in holding it hostage or using something important to her as leverage. I'm only interested in *her*—her happiness and her safety and her pleasure.

She doesn't meet my eyes as she takes the camera, and she turns back down the porch stairs after she takes it without another word.

"Ireland," I say in a strangled voice. "I was wrong. I was cruel. I'm sorry for it, and it won't ever happen again."

My words halt her progress, and she slowly pivots back to face me. The hurt and anger in her expression would be enough to drive back armies.

"You're goddamned right it's never happening again," she hisses. "Because I'm never coming back here. Ever. *Ever*."

Her words tear at me, tear at the part of me that wants her to feel safe. I should let her leave, and at this point, saying anything else aside from my apology is dangerously close to manipulation or coaxing, and I don't want that. I want her here because she wants to be here, not because she's guilted into it or convinces herself to stay against her better instincts.

That's what Caleb would do—clearly, that's what he *did*—given he's no longer here and Ireland is in possession of her car again. Ever the country gentleman, he escorted her to her car and honored her wishes the whole time.

I'm not Caleb.

I step down the stairs. "I don't want you to leave," I say in a low voice. She lifts her chin at me defiantly, refusing to step back as I approach.

"Then you shouldn't have *told* me to leave," she seethes.

"I shouldn't have," I agree.

"You treated me like shit for no reason," she continues, color rising in her cheeks, her eyes bright. "You made me feel stupid and awkward and embarrassed—and I don't deserve to feel any of those things!"

"Of course not," I murmur soothingly, because she's still letting me get closer and I don't want to spook her.

"I've spent so much of my life feeling like that, and I'm not going to feel like that anymore!" she says, blinking fast. Each blink feels like a blister rupturing open for me, knowing I'm the source of those tears. Shame and anger at myself stab deep, but I don't let it stop me from getting closer to her, close enough to reach out and stroke her cheek.

Her eyes flutter closed...and then snap back open. "Stop! You can't handsome your way out of this! You were an asshole!"

"I was."

"And you made me feel like I was the asshole!"

"I did."

A tear escapes one of her sweet blue eyes, and I catch it with my thumb. She bows her head slightly, as if defeated by the strength of her own emotions. "I'm so angry," she says to the ground. "I'm so furious with you. And I'm even more furious that I'm crying right now when all I want to do is yell at you."

"You can yell at me as much as you'd like," I tell her, sliding my hand to the nape of her neck while my thumb strokes along her cheek. "As long as you stay here to do it."

Another tear spills out. "I *want* to. Don't you see why it makes it extra awful? I want to stay here with you and Caleb so badly."

I don't miss how the present tense slips out in her words. A ray of hope shoots through me. "Stay, Ireland. Stay and let me make it up to you, make me suffer every minute you're due after what I did, just please"—I bend my face down and brush my lips against hers—"don't go."

She shivers at the touch of my mouth on hers. Parts her lips just enough to invite the gentle stroke of my tongue. And then we are kissing in truth, with her gathered in my arms and our slow kisses turning hot and sultry. Before long, my cock is burning against her belly and she's subtly rocking her hips against me.

When we part for air, her tears are gone, although her eyes are still vulnerable and glinting with turbulent feeling. "How?" she whispers. "How can you kiss me like this when just a couple hours ago...?"

I need to tell her about this part of me, but I don't want

it to sound like an excuse, like I'm justifying my awful actions because I've had awful things happen to me in the past. I press my forehead to hers and accept there's no easy way to talk about the busted parts of one's mind, the broken and the healing parts. "Did Caleb tell you I was in the army?"

"Yes," she answers softly. "Afghanistan. PTSD?"

"And a sprinkling of garden-variety depression and anxiety. It's—well, it's a work in progress. *I'm* a work in progress. I was already on the edge after seeing the town like that, but when I thought you might have died, when I saw you were in danger..." My fist is clenched in the material of her tank top at the small of her back, and I force myself to uncurl my fingers. "We went through so many villages that looked exactly like that. Just heaps of stones and bricks. And you never knew what would happen when you were walking through. Would you be shot at? Step on an IED? Find the bodies of a dead family left out in the sun? It's like being turned up to maximum volume for hours...days. And then the volume knob breaks clean off and you can't turn it down anymore."

I stare at her, letting her see something I've only ever let Caleb see. Me, as I am, part shell and part sensitive boy who got beat to shit after school every day. "I'm so sorry, Ireland. I didn't want to hurt you. I wanted you *safe*...and I was so desperate to get you away from anything unsafe that I hurt you to do it. It's unforgivable, and I know that... I just also want you to know *why*. It's not because I don't want you or care for you. Just the fucking opposite."

Her eyes are huge and liquid, like deep-blue waters of emotion, and her lower lip trembles the slightest bit as she asks, "How can I trust you won't be awful to me again?"

All over again, I'm stabbed with shame and regret and self-directed fury. I know it's not helpful—I've spent the last five years listening to therapists and other veterans *tell* me it's not helpful—but the shame comes all the same.

And yet with it comes the faintest note of something else. Hope? Optimism?

Certainty?

Yes, I think, *it's because I'm certain about Ireland.* I've never had a reason to believe in things like fate or destiny—the war was very effective at proving there's nothing but chaos in this world—but Ireland makes me doubt all that now.

"Because you're mine."

Her eyes flick over my face, searching me. "You mean that?"

My hold tightens on her. "Yes, baby. You're mine and Caleb's, and you'll remain ours until you don't want to be any longer."

"Yours." She tries out the word, as if the entire concept is foreign to her. As if no one's ever tried to possess her before.

Then they were all fucking fools.

"Ours," I confirm roughly, yanking her close once again. "As long as you want us."

She nibbles on her lower lip, and I can't help it. I bend down and bite that lip for her. "Do you still want us, Ireland?" I murmur against her mouth. "Will you stay and let me make it up to you?"

CHAPTER THIRTEEN

IRELAND

A couple of years ago, I was watching a movie with a handful of girlfriends as we traded gossip and passed around popcorn and bottles of wine. And we got to the part of the movie where the hero makes his grand gesture, chasing after the heroine and declaring his love for her. Declaring that she was *his*.

The room gave a collective groan at this, popcorn flying at the screen, and someone pronounced how utterly backward and chauvinistic that was and how she'd never be caught dead with a man who looked at her and said *mine*. A man who looked at her like she was a prize in the machine simply waiting to be claimed.

I stayed silent.

Because I wasn't going to argue that on a structural level men should act proprietary with women, and I never would. But on a personal level, well...

It was hard to look at my friend, who was slender and sleek and would no doubt have men wanting her everywhere she went and not think *easy for you to say*. Her body was the kind of body that people wanted to claim, wanted to stake some kind of sexual ownership of, and mine was not—never had been, and as years of pointless diet torture had taught me, never would be.

So it was hard not to *wish* I had the luxury of scoffing at male desire. It was hard to watch those movies and know that, according to them, people like me didn't have heroes chasing after them. People like me are the best friends, the comic relief, maybe even the villain.

And in real life? In real life, the kind of male attention I received was dangerous and demeaning. Aggressive frat boys who told me I should feel "lucky" to have them fuck me and then got belligerent and nasty when I refused them. Mean men at bars who grabbed and groped and assumed I'd be grateful for the assault since clearly nobody else would ever want to touch my body.

Girls like me, we didn't get chased, we didn't get claimed, we didn't get the happily ever after. Not in movies. Not in real life.

And was it such a crime to want those things? I burned to have them, ached to be the heroine standing in the rain or at the airport or whatever while the hero pleaded and begged and humbled himself for the privilege and honor to be with me. While he ached and burned for my attention and my body.

And now here I am, listening to Ben plead and beg. Listening to him lay his claim.

Mine. Ours.

The corollary to Ben's words darts around my mind, and it swallows up every other wound and worry: *Theirs.*

I've never belonged to another person before, not in the way that Ben is implying. Even Brian always made sure to tell people we were friends with benefits—or worse. At one memorably shameful work event, he told his boss I was his cousin in town for the week.

So, no, I've never had someone stand in front of me, eyes blazing with possessive lust, and practically vibrate with the need to claim me. Declare I'm *theirs*.

I've never been the heroine. Until now...and God help me, I like it. I like having this man on his proverbial knees while he also looks like he wants nothing more than to pin me against my own car and fuck me until the only word I remember is his name.

"Please, Ireland," Ben says, his voice hoarse and his eyes swirling with a mixture of desperation and lust that my body can't help but answer. "Please."

I suck in a breath, my anger blowing away into nothing. "You have to promise to treat me with dignity," I say, sliding my hands up his chest. "You can't hurt me again."

"Never again," he vows, and then his lips are tracing back over mine with hungry, greedy kisses. "God, Ireland, never fucking again."

He wraps my hand in one of his big ones and tugs me inside the house with the kind of uncompromising urgency that brooks no argument. Not that I'd argue anyway. There's something about having a six-foot-plus, square-jawed, dark-eyed soldier yank you up to his bed that makes a girl eager.

But he surprises me—he takes me to Caleb's bed instead, sitting back against the headboard with his long, muscular legs sprawled.

"Shorts off, panties off," he says. It's not a question.

"What about you?" I ask in a breathy voice.

Ben holds up a hand at my question, as if to say *in a minute*, even though I can see his thick erection stretching all the way to his hip and would hazard a guess *it* doesn't want to wait for any period of time. "Sit after you get bare for me. We're going to give Caleb a treat when he gets home."

God, yes.

I swallow with a combination of nervousness and arousal, but I've already gone to work on my buttons and zipper. As soon as I'm as Ben wants, naked from the waist down and settling between his legs, he finally answers my question. "Don't worry, baby. I'll get what I need very soon."

He arranges me with all the bossy precision of a field commander used to having his orders followed. I'm leaned back against his broad chest and my legs are arranged to drape over his in a way that exposes my pussy to the open air. I almost have a moment of self-consciousness when I feel how wide Ben's legs have to part to accommodate my ass, but it's erased the moment I hear his moan as his erection makes contact with my body. His control fractures the tiniest bit, and he pushes his swollen cock against the place where the small of my back curves into my naked bottom.

"Fuck yes," he grates in my ear. "I love your body. Caleb does too—should we get that pussy of yours ready for him?"

"Yes," I whisper, already wet from Caleb's earlier attention and now from the kiss of cool air along my intimate places. But then Ben strokes a hand down over my breast, over the slopes of my stomach, and down to my feminine place, and I instantly grow even wetter.

"Oh baby," he rumbles. "You need us right now, don't you? Need your boys to take care of that pretty little cunt?"

My head drops back onto his shoulder as his finger delves inside. "Yes," I moan. "I need it." And even just the thought of Ben and Caleb sliding their throbbing columns of unyielding flesh inside me is enough to make me clamp down on Ben's finger. He gives an answering growl.

"Careful, baby," he murmurs. "I'm not letting you come until Caleb gets here. It's going to be a long dance at the edge if you keep up like this."

But what choice do I have? With a handsome, tortured soldier holding me close with one arm while his other reaches between my legs to play with me as if I'm his new toy? What girl wouldn't already be on the edge?

"God, I love how you open up like a flower," he groans, his finger tracing my swelling, slick folds. He buries his nose in my neck and breathes me in. "You're perfect. Fucking perfect."

I'm nearly beyond speech with wanting his fingers to do more. "Ben…" is all I can manage, and then I'm just whimpering and squirming as he teases the pad of one finger around my budding clitoris.

Behind me, I can feel the heat of his erection even through his jeans, like a rod of scorching need. I want it *inside* me— anywhere, everywhere. And just the thought of having him *everywhere* launches me that much closer to orgasm.

"Ben," I beg. "Don't make me wait any longer."

"You'll wait as long as I say you will," he replies in that dark, authoritative voice that never fails to make me quiver in delight. "Even if it's *hours*."

Hours?

And to prove his point, he trails his touch away from my clit...down, down, down.

"Oh!" I gasp as he presses against a place no one's ever touched before. His finger is slick with where it's been, and it easily penetrates the tight ring of muscle there. I writhe against the new pressure and the illicit thrill of it, and Ben ducks his mouth to my ear. "You want me to fuck you here? Caleb too?" His finger probes deeper, and I make a helpless noise of assent. "What about both of us at the same time, hmm? Working both your tight holes while you're pinned helpless between us?"

"Yes," I whimper, and he rewards me with the heel of his palm against my clit as he carefully fingers my ass. I'm so needful that his entire hand is now wet with me, and playing with my ass clearly gets Ben beyond needful too, because he grinds out several curse words as his other hand flies to his pants to free his cock so it can rub along my bare skin.

And that's how Caleb finds us just a few moments later— me shamelessly rocking against his best friend's hand, my dirtiest secrets penetrated and exposed for viewing, and Ben's erection grinding livid and hot against my skin.

Caleb stands in the doorway of his room, looking staggered. He runs a shaking hand over his mouth, his green eyes flickering back and forth between Ben and me, between the wet and ready place between my legs and the slow grind of Ben's hips against my ass.

"Peach," Caleb breathes, as if he can hardly believe I'm here, and my heart seizes. If I can forgive Ben for pushing me away, I can forgive Caleb for letting me go. In fact, I feel like

I can forgive them for *anything*, so long as they finally fuck me. So long as I get to live out Ben's filthy suggestion and experience what it's like to be completely filled. What it's like to have both of them inside me at the same time.

"Caleb," I say, reaching for him, and he's suddenly unfrozen, racing to the bed as he tears off his clothes.

"I wouldn't let her come until you got here," Ben says with a trace of smugness. "She's so fucking wet for you."

Caleb finally kicks off his jeans and boxers and puts a knee up on the bed. My mouth goes dry at the sight of him—all that heavy muscle coiled tight with the need to fuck, those hands twitching at his sides like it's taking everything he has not to grab me and pull me right onto his turgid length. The length that now bobs proudly from his hips, the end of it shiny and tight and beginning to glisten for me at the tip, even though he's only just now joined us.

And when he crawls into the opening made by my legs hooked over Ben's, I can't resist the urge to touch him. To run my fingers over those bulging muscles and the light-brown hair that dusts over his chest and abs. He groans at my touch and then leans forward to nuzzle my breasts, turning his head to bite at the tender undersides through the fabric. It's raw and animalistic and even more so while another man is playing with my asshole as he does it.

Caleb lifts his head to look at Ben. "You said her pussy is ready for me?"

"See for yourself," Ben says and moves his hand to the side—but keeps his middle finger firmly inside my other entrance.

Caleb sucks in a breath. "Holy fuck," he mutters and then glances over to my face, where he no doubt can guess from my flushed cheeks and hooded eyes how much I like what Ben's doing. "Holy fuck," he repeats, this time to himself, as if he can't believe his luck.

I crane my own head now to look up at Ben. His jaw is working tight and his eyebrows are pulled together in strain, like it's taking everything he has not to be fucking me right now. "Are you going to fuck me there?" I ask shyly. "Now?"

He looks down at me, eyes glinting. "Do you want me to fuck you there? Now?"

"Yes," I say with a blush. "But...I haven't done it before."

"Ben is very good at it," Caleb says and then flushes deeply. I decide I want very much to hear more about this and how Caleb knows—and maybe have some demonstrations—but then Ben is sliding out from behind me and stalking to his room, his erection jutting up in a deliciously thick arc from his parted jeans. He returns without his shirt and with a handful of supplies.

"Lie down, Ireland," he commands. I notice his hands are trembling as he hooks his thumbs in the waistband of his jeans and pulls them off, and the evidence of his desire inflames me. Reassures me, even though I'm a little nervous about what comes next.

I move to the middle of the bed as Caleb easily rolls a condom over himself and joins me. He rolls me to my side so we face each other, and he runs the back of his fingers over my face.

"I'm so glad you're here," he says, and there's no mistaking the tenderness in his voice, the depth in his eyes.

Unexpectedly, emotion knots in my throat. "Really?" I whisper. "We only had one night together. If I'd left, it wouldn't have been that big of a deal."

Caleb's already shaking his head. "It would've been. I know it hasn't been long, but can't you feel it?"

"It?" I echo, and he takes my hand and splays it over his chest. Underneath my palm, his heart beats warm and steady and fast.

"Yes," he says solemnly. "It."

My lips part, but I'm not sure what to say. Because I do feel *it*, and if the boys feel it too...

Well, it makes me feel something I've never really felt before. Optimistic and confident and happy and...

Loved.

As if to shore up Caleb's sweet words, Ben kisses my shoulder from behind me and then brushes his lips over the shell of my ear.

"I feel the same way, Ireland. You're ours."

Theirs.

"Yes," I say almost dizzily. "I feel it. I'm yours."

What else can be said after that? Caleb reaches down between my legs to test my readiness and groans at what he finds. With a big callused hand, he pulls my knee up to his hip, and then I feel the broad head of his penis probing slick and latex-covered at my seam.

"Shit," he mumbles as he works the tip of his dick inside me. "Shit, Ireland, you feel so good."

I squirm on the end of his cock, trying to feed more into

my body, and he gives a breathless laugh. "I got you, peach, hold on. Trust me to give you what you need."

"Want it *now*," I growl, and he laughs some more.

"Ben, how long did you tease her for?"

"Not very long," is the amused answer. "But you remember how responsive she is."

Caleb's eyes light back on my face, and his laughing mouth pulls into a wicked smile. "I do remember." And with a thrust of his muscled ass, he plows all the way home.

My fingernails dig into his shoulders as my sex stretches and ripples around him, and he gives me three deep and grinding strokes in return, the pressure of his thickness inside me and the gorgeous friction against my clit sending me over the edge. The tension inside my body shatters into a mosaic of delicious sensation—seizing waves low in my belly, flutters of pure pleasure radiating from my clit, tingles of electricity shooting down to the pads of my fingers and the bottoms of my toes.

"Fuck," Caleb groans, his head dropping back. "She's coming already. I can feel it. *Fuck*."

Ben bites me on the shoulder with a pleased rumble. "Good. Come hard for Caleb, baby. Get all nice and tight for us."

His dirty words spur me on, and my head is tossing on the bed as I ride out my climax on his glorious organ. Caleb is gritting his teeth in order to keep from following me, and then we both let out agonized gasps as Ben's slick finger finds my pleated entrance once again and pushes inside.

"Oh God," I pant, my orgasm surging hard again from the

extra stimulation. "Oh God, oh God."

"You better hurry," Caleb grinds out. "I'm not going to last much longer."

"Then how are you going to last when it's my cock pushing inside her?" Ben asks.

Caleb shivers at his words, biting off a curse as he no doubt imagines how it will feel, how tight I'll get with another huge shaft wedged inside me.

My orgasm finally subsides, leaving me limp and quivering, and Ben adds a second finger. "Push against my touch," he advises as I tense up. "It'll open you more to me. Good girl, that's it. Do you feel dirty with my fingers in your ass? Do you feel sexy?"

I give it a couple of breaths, adjusting slowly to the foreign feeling. It does feel dirty, it does feel sexy, especially when I see Caleb gazing at me with an expression bordering on awestruck as he slowly glides his girth in and out of me in time to Ben's pumping fingers. Especially when I look up at Ben and see a man who's about to tear the bed apart with his teeth if he isn't inside my body right this minute.

"I'm ready," I murmur up to him, turning as much as I can to look at the irresistible man kneeling behind me. "I'm ready for you."

"Are you sure?" he asks, and I can see the toll it takes on him to proceed with care. To delay. His shoulders are shaking, the muscles of his belly are clenched so tightly that every band and slab is etched in high relief and glistening with sweat. His cock is dark and distended. A large vein traces up the side, and the slit at his crown is wet and shining with pre-come. "I'll be careful with you, Ireland, I swear to God."

"I know," I say, giving him a sated smile. I'm still dizzy with all the hormones from my last climax. "And I'm sure."

He drops another kiss on my shoulder and then reaches for a condom, tearing the packet open with his teeth and sheathing himself in a quick, practiced movement. There's the click of a bottle cap, and then Caleb and I are treated to the sight of Ben spreading lube down the length of his rigid erection. Through the glisten of the latex and lubricant, I can still see all the veins and the plump crown in perfect detail, and my body craves it, longs for it, even though I have one hot erection already lodged inside my body.

"Same as before," Ben says, tossing the closed lube bottle to the side of the bed. "It's just like my fingers."

"He's lying," Caleb says, his dimple peeking out from under his beard.

"Okay, I'm lying a little," Ben amends. "It's just like my fingers...if my fingers were much, much bigger."

He lies down so the muscled length of his body stretches out behind mine. I feel another flash of bashful unease—there's something about having his firm chest and abs and thighs pressed against the soft gradients and creases of my back and bottom that brings up my worst feelings about my body. Between Caleb at my front and Ben at my back, there's no angle I can twist myself to try to make my waist look smaller, no hiding the crease between my stomach and my hip, no attempting to make my FUPA look smoother. There's no hiding the dimples in my bottom and thighs. I'm completely exposed, naked and squeezed between two men who could be on the cover of a magazine.

But my chagrin vanishes the moment Ben presses fully against me and lets out a groan that goes up to the rafters.

"*Fuck*," he curses, unable to stop himself from stroking his cock along the seam of my backside. "I'm never letting you leave this bed."

I look back to Caleb, who seems to have the same idea, judging by his bitten lower lip and his roaming, grasping hands.

What girl would ever *want* to leave this bed? Between these two?

"I'm never going anywhere else ever again," I say with a half laugh that turns into a half gasp as I feel the broad tip of him press against my opening. "Oh, Ben."

"Gonna fuck you so good," he husks. "So good, baby."

The hoarse urgency in his voice is an aphrodisiac all its own—not that I need one with the two of them around. I'm so wet that whenever Caleb gives me a thrust, it's like a hot knife moving through butter, and I can feel the beginning of another climax twining into a tight knot right behind my clitoris.

The pressure as Ben begins to work his way into the small aperture is intense—intense enough that I bury my face in Caleb's strong chest as I try to catch my breath.

"Shh," Caleb soothes, stroking my hair and my arm. "This is the hardest part. You just have to breathe."

I breathe as he instructs, trying to push against Ben's invasion, but he's so big, so wide, and there's a pinching feeling that borders on pain as he finally works his way past my rings of muscle.

"*Tight*," Ben grunts, shoving in another inch. "Fucking tight."

I press my face harder against Caleb, telling myself *breathe breathe breathe,* and Caleb runs a gentling palm over my thigh and hip, his other arm underneath me and holding me close to him.

Ben curls a hand around my hip and uses another to anchor my shoulder, and then he gives me a final shove that rips the breath right from my body and sends him as deep as he can go.

"Are you okay?" he asks in a strained voice. I can feel him trembling and sweating with the effort to hold his body still, and when I pull my head back and see Caleb, I see the same strain stamped all over him too.

"A moment," I choke out, my entire body tense and aching with the invasion of not one but two massive erections. "Need a moment."

Now firmly in place, Ben readjusts so he's pressed all against me again, and he nuzzles my neck, my hair, my shoulder. Like an animal gentling its mate. And he praises me, telling me how sweet I am, how beautiful I am, how good I make him feel. He promises to make me feel good too. He promises I can use his body and Caleb's to sate my lusts any time I want.

He says I'm the sexiest woman in the world, and Caleb murmurs his agreement, kissing my mouth as Ben kisses the nape of my neck.

As they both throb inside me.

A minute passes, and then another, and between the kissing and the praising, the discomfort has melted away. Instead, I feel gloriously, happily *full.* Complete, even. Like this is the way I'm meant to have sex, like I was formed at birth to mold between these two men.

"Okay," I say, still a bit shaky but also aroused beyond all belief and ready for the climax that's waiting just a few thrusts away. "More, please." I think of what I said last night and smile. "*All of it.*"

"We're gonna give you all of it," says Caleb with a filthy gleam in his eye. "You better hold on tight, little peach."

Together they begin fucking me with careful, rolling thrusts, both of them completely attuned to me, watching and listening with an attentiveness that can only be called reverent. When I flinch, they pause and adjust the angles of their hips until I sigh again. When I gasp, they kiss and lick my mouth and neck until I'm squirming down onto them. And when I dig my fingernails into Caleb's shoulder and moan, they reward me with deep, railing thrusts that leave me seeing stars and panting their names.

My hovering orgasm only needs a few minutes of this to finally explode into release. With an unladylike moan, I detonate around the two cocks buried inside me. Hard, clenching contractions take me, make everything below my navel feel like a giant squeezing fist of pure pleasure, and I'm dimly aware my orgasm is driving the men wild.

Ben and Caleb link hands over my hip to hold me steady as I writhe through the delight, and together they surge into me as deep as they can.

"Gonna come...so hard," pants Caleb, and behind me, I hear Ben grunt in agreement. Then Caleb lets out an almighty yell, his head thrown back and the cords in his neck straining, and heat scalds my sheath through the condom after he pumps waves of his orgasm into the latex.

It triggers more pleasure of my own, and stars dance at the edge of my vision as a delicate pain lights up nerve endings everywhere on my body. Ben's sunk his teeth into my neck and, with a bitten-off noise, erupts otherwise silently against the tight, dirty glove of my channel, filling his own condom with spurt after spurt of hot seed.

Both of them keep thrusting through their ejaculations, and I keep undulating between them as my own climax ebbs gradually into satisfied exhaustion. In a tangle of arms, I'm cradled between them, and we're sweaty and the condoms need to be taken care of, and I have no doubt I'm going to be sore, but at this moment, all I can think is what I told them earlier.

I'm never going anywhere else again.

Yes, they were sex words, but I realize they're also true in every other sense as well. I want to stay.

I'm *going* to stay.

CHAPTER FOURTEEN

CALEB

The sun blazes nosy and chiding through the window, reminding us there's so much to do and fix outside these walls, but we ignore it, spending the afternoon as if it's the dead of night—doing all manner of wicked and depraved things normally saved for hours of darkness.

After we clean up, Ben and I spend a long time between Ireland's legs, jostling for space and the chance to lick at her sweet honey. And after she comes twice more, we once again cradle her between us and take her at the same time. This time, I'm the one fucking her tight, rear hole, and the grip of her is insane. And with the pressure from Ben's cock inside her pussy and the added stimulation of feeling him stroke against me through her thin walls, it's a miracle I last long enough to make sure she comes first. Somehow I manage it, lips thin and eyes shut, waiting until the last of her shudders die down before I open my eyes and let myself just *look* at her writhing between us. Those sweet slopes and tucks of her body. The way her curves yield softly to my form as I move against her. The way her body spills out of my hands as I fondle and squeeze at her.

She's straight out of my wet dreams, out of every fantasy

I've ever had—dark hair soft as silk and flowing like water over Ben's arm. Blue eyes to rival the storm-cleansed sky outside. Perfectly formed lips that beg for my own.

And a body like those paintings in art class—with soft rolls and a round bottom and a plump little pussy that all but begs to be fucked and fucked thoroughly.

That's all it takes, looking at her, and I come with a bellow and a bowing body, pumping my condom full of hot, slick seed. Ben watches me roar and tense through it, and then he takes Ireland's mouth in a searing kiss as he follows me over the edge with a single quiet noise.

We've always used condoms with every woman we've been with, always, always, and a jolt of fresh blood hits my spent cock as I think about what it would be like to skip the condoms next time. To claim this beautiful woman from the inside out, to feel the slippery heat of Ben doing the same.

My cock gives another pulse, trying valiantly to rise to the occasion, and Ireland gives me a happy, if slightly rueful, smile.

"I need a break, cowboy," she says, wincing a bit as we tug free of her body. "Another few minutes, at least."

"We have all the time in the world," Ben says. His brows draw together as he gazes down at her. "I hope."

For a moment she doesn't answer, simply searching Ben's face and then mine as if trying to read our thoughts. Apparently satisfied by what she sees, she gives us a lazy nod, like a queen.

"All the time in the world."

◆ ◆ ◆ ◆

When late afternoon begins to crest into evening, we drive

back to Holm. Ben needs to start making calls and contacting insurance companies about the tavern, and after making sure Mrs. Parry and Mrs. Harthcock are safe and settled, I'm anxious to get back to town to help in whatever way I can.

To our surprise, Ireland is just as eager to go. She changes into fresh clothes and slings her camera around her shoulder.

"What?" she asks, catching Ben and me looking at her.

"You don't have to come," I tell her gently. "It's not your town, and anyway, I don't know how much there will be to do—"

"There will be plenty to do, for one thing, and for another, while this may not be my home, it *is* yours. I'm not a totally heartless city girl; I want to help, and I can help, and I'm coming along too. So long as it won't be hard on Ben."

Ben crosses over to her and yanks her close. "I swear it won't be," he murmurs, training those intense, dark eyes on Ireland's mouth. And then he gives her a kiss like he's just come home from the war all over again.

Holm is flooded with people when we get there—police cars and pickup trucks crowd the debris-choked streets—but Ireland is right. Even with so many people here, there's plenty to do. While Ben focuses on the tavern, Ireland and I spend the next five or six hours working to help shift rubble and sort through wreckage. We work deep into the humid dark, Greta sticking close and providing moral support by licking everyone's hands and doing enough tail-wagging for an entire pack of dogs. And Ireland frequently pauses in order to snap pictures of the town at work righting itself.

I don't know much about photography beyond taking

pictures of used farm equipment to sell it on the internet, but even I can see her pictures are striking. An older woman crying in front of the flattened house where her sister died. Dirt-streaked faces gazing out at the sunset. Ben, head bowed in misery as he stands in the doorway of the tavern.

The pictures give me chills, and as we're sitting around the kitchen table, each with a well-earned glass of bourbon as the night presses in through the windows, I ask her, "Why didn't you become a photographer for real? Why go work for Drew?" I like Drew quite a lot, but that doesn't mean Ireland isn't wasted writing tweets for microbreweries or creating brand strategy for a sandwich chain. Pictures like these could be in newspapers, on the covers of magazines; she could be anywhere, with her pick of people wanting her pictures.

Ireland takes a long drink of bourbon and reaches out to idly finger a sunflower sitting in an old jelly jar on the table. I saw the bloom as we walked in, still fresh and healthy and sheltered from the storm by the porch stairs—knowing Ireland's fascination with them, I made sure to come out and pick it for her while she got cleaned up. I'm glad I did, because watching her face soften as she studies the flower makes my chest puff out with pride. "I, uh, I turned down a photography scholarship in college," she says eventually, eyes still on the flower. "And decided to stay local. Major in something more practical."

It sounds plausible enough—hell, I did the same, choosing a college only two hours away so I could be close to the farm while I got my degree in Ag Econ—but there's something about the way she doesn't look at us as she answers that makes me think there's more to the story than she's willing to share right now.

She's saved from me pressing further by Ben's stifled yawn, and we abandon our bourbon for a shower and sleep. Ben surprises me by climbing into bed with us, folding Ireland into his big arms, and reaching out with one foot to touch mine like we used to do when we were boys sharing a bed. But when I stir in the middle of the night, I find Ireland in my arms instead, my foot encountering nothing but cool sheets under her tucked-up legs.

He still doesn't trust himself to sleep with us the whole night through.

◆ ◆ ◆ ◆

"...haven't talked to them yet at all. I wanted to ask you first, of course."

Ireland's voice filters through my groggy brain, and I roll over to see her perched on the edge of the bed, her legs curled up beside her, a phone to her ear. Like this, the mouthwatering angles of her hips and ass are perfectly delineated by the morning sunshine pouring in through the window. I move closer to her and start shamelessly squeezing her curves and stroking her stomach. She ineffectively bats at me as she keeps talking.

"I'm so glad you like them, and we're going back today, so I'll take more. I think this is a much stronger pitch in the long run, but I'll need to come back a few more times. I want to capture all the rebuilding efforts and stuff like that."

I hear Drew's voice on the other end, but I ignore it, busy

exploring Ireland's body and teasing fingers over her hip to the soft vee of her pussy.

She gives a delicious shiver, and her voice when she answers her boss is a little strained. "Yes, let's make sure to add this to the meeting tomorrow. I want everybody's feedback."

They exchange a few more words before she hangs up, and I curl my hand possessively over my new favorite toy.

"You're going back to Kansas City," I say. I knew she'd have to, but I can't fight the irrational urge to truss her up to my bed and keep her here at the farm forever.

She sighs and parts her legs enough for me to pet her cunt properly. "I'll leave tonight, since my meeting is first thing tomorrow. I'm going to see if we can pitch a different angle to the Tourism Board. Rather than 'farmers at work' for *Real Kansas*, I want to show Holm. The citizens working together after the storm, grieving together and helping each other."

I think of her pictures last night, of the goose bumps they gave me, and make an approving noise. "I like that idea."

"So does Drew, so it's really down to convincing the client. At any rate," Ireland says, her eyes shyly glancing away, "Drew thinks I should sell some of the pictures too. He's reaching out to his friends at some local and national papers now."

"That's wonderful!" I slide my arms around her and tug her even closer so I can reward this good news with more caresses and strokes where she's growing wet and needy. "Your pictures should be in every paper, in every magazine."

"You're just saying that because you want to have sex with me again," she mutters, but she blushes.

"No, I'm saying that *and* I want to have sex with you again.

Now, I'm going to holler for Ben, and when he gets in here, I suggest you be ready."

◆ ◆ ◆ ◆

Watching Ireland leave is painful, even with as tired as Ben and I are from working in town all day. We each kiss her senseless before she climbs into the car, crowding her against the car door and taking turns with her lush mouth until we're all breathless and she can barely stand.

"Come back to us," I plead against her lips.

"You're ours," Ben says simply, and then he leans down and bites at her neck. She shudders against us.

"Yours." She smiles. "I'm yours."

She calls us every night, and for once, the internet connection at the farmhouse is strong enough for the three of us to use video chat for its best purpose—so she can see Ben and me stroke off for her while she leisurely fingerfucks herself. From her calls, we also learn the Tourism Board is thrilled about the new pitch and that the *Kansas City Star* has been running her pictures with the promise to buy more.

She awkwardly, adorably, asks if she can come visit this weekend.

"How about you move in," Ben says.

She laughs, but I know he's not joking. The time away from her has done nothing to dull our certainty that she's our girl, the missing piece to our hearts, and every moment she's away from us is painful. After she offhandedly mentions being able to work remotely, it makes it impossible not to dream and hope of a time when she can stay here always. But Ben and I agree not to push her too fast. We've had years and years to adjust to the way we like our love and our sex, but Ireland's only had a week.

We can be patient. Maybe.

When she returns on Friday afternoon in her gravel-dusted Prius and with a fresh coat of lavender lipstick on that irresistible mouth, Ben and I are waiting.

She parks in the driveway and climbs out of the car, looking a bit shy, like she's not sure what it will be like to be with us in person again. She's wearing another pencil skirt, this time with heels and a clingy cardigan thing that shows off all my favorite parts of her breasts and stomach and waist. The pencil skirt hugs her tightly enough that I can easily perceive the inverted triangle of her crotch, and even though I was already hard with anticipation simply knowing she was on the way, seeing her in the flesh is like a kick of heat right to my dick. My balls tighten and my shaft swells even more, needing to be buried inside her at the first opportunity.

Ben is the first to move, prowling toward her like a wolf and then seizing her in a lewd kiss that has her nipples poking through her sweater.

"Inside," he growls, all beast to Ireland's beauty. "Fucking *now*."

We go inside, and we fuck Ireland in her pencil skirt, and then in nothing but her heels, and then again in nothing but her lipstick.

"Move in," Ben says again as we all lie in bed that night, naked and sweaty and spent.

Ireland laughs again, burrowing into us and falling asleep

in a record amount of time.

This time, Ben almost manages to stay the entire night with us before creeping back to his own bed where he feels safe.

CHAPTER FIFTEEN

IRELAND

"No way," I say firmly. "Uh-uh. Nothing doing."

It's my fourth weekend with the boys—*my* boys—and the miserable August heat has driven us to the big farm pond at the back of the property. I thought we were heading back here simply to sit beside the water and let the breeze cool us off, but that notion evaporated the minute we reached the small wooden dock and both Caleb and Ben stripped completely naked. I barely had a chance to ogle their big, muscled bodies with those delightfully taut asses and heavy, semihard cocks, before they launched themselves into the water.

Completely naked.

"Come on, peach!" Caleb says with his customary grin. "It feels amazing!"

I shake my head vigorously. It's hot as hell out here, and while I normally love swimming, I love swimming in a *swimsuit*. One that has been carefully selected to support and flatter. The idea of stripping naked in all this bright sunlight, every wobbly inch of me exposed, and then jumping into the water with all those wobbly inches at maximum wobble is enough to make me wince.

It's strange, because a month ago, I would have avowed the new Ireland was confident and fierce and no longer cared about wobbles at all. And you would think having two hunky farm boys jumping my bones every few hours would have cured me of any insecurity at all!

I'm annoyed with myself about it. It feels like I'm going backward...and with no good reason. These boys adore me. I adore them. They've never done anything to make me feel anything *but* the sexiest woman alive.

But, if I'm honest, when Ben and I fought and I left, there was this tiny part of me that said, *Oh. Of course. What did I expect would happen? Plus-sized girls don't date cute, fit guys. Men like them won't want to keep you around.*

I know it was his war trauma talking, and Ben never made that moment about my body—but I did. I definitely did. And there's this weird little place in my mind that won't let go of it, like a dog with a bone. Just chewing over this insecurity until it's gross and splintery and rank. Until it whispers things like *how long do you really think this can last? How long until they* really *look at your body and decide not to want you anymore?*

"I don't like swimming with fish," I lie, sitting on the dock instead. I stretch out my legs and smooth my skirt primly down my thighs. The fabric sticks to my skin because I'm so sweaty, and I try not to think about how cold the swimming hole looks right now. How refreshing. "I prefer to swim in clean water. Without living things in it."

"The fish are very nice fish," Caleb promises. "They haven't eaten a person in years."

"Funny," I reply. "Very funny. I'm still not coming in."

"I think you are," Ben says from next to the dock. The water flows gracefully over his strong shoulders as he effortlessly treads in place, the tantalizing lines of his firm body disappearing into the green depths and hiding the most interesting parts from view.

I try to catch a glimpse anyway.

I bet even the cool water swallowing up his body is doing nothing to diminish that perfect penis of his.

Caleb is the first to haul himself up the dock ladder, but Ben follows right after, and then I don't have to crane my neck anymore to see their beautiful cocks because they're right in front of me.

"No," I say, having a feeling where this is going. "I'm not going in."

"You're all flushed, peach," Caleb coaxes. Even as he says the words, a drop of sweat drips down from my hairline. "A nice dip would make you feel better."

Ben just stares down at me with that penetrating way of his, like he can see all the things I don't want him to see.

I look away, pretending to fuss with the hem of my skirt and also pretending my dress isn't sweat-soaked and clinging to my back because I'm dying in the sun. "I'm not actually that hot," I fib. "The breeze off the water is enough to cool me down."

Ben drops to his knees and moves over me so he's straddling my legs. He plants his hands on either side of my hips and leans forward, his lips grazing my jaw. "If you don't get into the water, I'm pulling you in."

I narrow my eyes. "You wouldn't."

He shrugs without answering, leaning in to kiss my neck, heedless of the sweat there.

"You monster," I accuse. "What if I can't swim?"

At this he pulls back and searches my face. "But you can swim, can't you? This isn't about swimming at all. There's something else holding you back."

He's so close and so beautiful and his expression is unnervingly kind. I can't keep looking at him; the gross little voice in my head won't let me.

"Ireland," Ben warns. "Talk or be thrown in."

"I'm not doing either—"

With a movement so quick I barely see it, he's on his feet and has one of my hands while Caleb has the other. I'm yanked up, and before I can catch my balance, I'm in the water, my toes touching soft, cool mud before I kick back up to the surface, spluttering.

They stand naked above me, looking very proud of themselves. "There," Caleb says, laughter in his voice. "That wasn't so bad, was it? Aren't you cooler now?"

"This dress is dry-clean only, you dicks," I grouse. But I can't lie... The water does feel good.

"Now that it's all wet, you should take it off," Caleb suggests. His cock seems to agree, thickening as he peers down at me in the water. "Your underthings too. You know, in case they're also dry-clean only."

I think for a moment. I can't help but be squeamish about the idea of stripping in the bright, unforgiving light of the summer sun, but if I get in the water right away, maybe it won't feel so exposing...

I swim toward the ladder and pull myself up, and before I can reach for my zipper, Caleb and Ben are helping me unzip and peel off the wet dress. I shoo them away out of instinct, and with schoolboy laughing and whooping, they jump back into the water.

Too late I realize my mistake. Right next to me, they wouldn't have been able to properly see my body, but now that they're back in the water, I'm totally exposed again. It's like being on a fucking runway, and their view up at me is far from the ideal angle.

Just finish undressing quickly and get down the ladder, I coach myself, turning away before I unhook my bra. Then I discover facing away from them means they'll see more of the cellulite on my ass and on the backs of my thighs—but being in profile means they'll see my belly. Facing them means they'll see my breasts under the cruel duress of gravity.

Fuck.

But when I drop the bra and turn, I don't see two pairs of judgmental eyes cataloging my every stretch mark and dimple. Instead, both men have swum to the edge of the dock and are watching me with hot gazes full of hunger. One of Caleb's hands is moving lazily under the water, and I flush when I realize what he's doing.

"Now your panties," Ben grates out. He's breathing hard as he watches me. "Those too."

Their hungry stares fill me with power, and my insecurity melts away as if it were never there. I shimmy out of my panties and even give a little hip swivel as I do.

"Fuck me," Caleb groans. "Get in here, peach. Now."

I do. I run and jump in, wobbles forgotten, and later that afternoon, when the three of us fuck under the shade of a big cottonwood tree, I can't even remember what it feels like to be embarrassed at all.

◆ ◆ ◆ ◆

The nightlight in Caleb's room is for Ben.

I have this epiphany as I'm gently turned into Caleb's arms and Ben slides out of the bed to go to his room.

The nightlight is so Ben can find his way in the dark.

Away from us.

My heart squeezes as I press my face into Caleb's warm chest and let the steady swell of his breathing lull me back to sleep.

I wake alone in the morning, which is normal for us. Ben never sleeps the whole night in here, and Caleb gets up around dawn to tend to the farm. I stretch and sigh at the darkened nightlight. I want Ben to stay the night with us. His bed is only a twin—something I think was an intentional choice, meaning no one could ever sleep in his bed with him—so it has to be Caleb's bed. I wish there was a way to tell him I'd be happy to sleep with lights on, the television on, anything he needed, without it becoming awkward, but I can't think of the right words. The words to reassure him that I don't think he's broken or damaged, that I simply want to share everything with him. Sleep included.

I'm going to talk to him about it, I decide as I shower and get dressed. *Today*. If it's nightmares, then we'll work through it. If it's space, then I'll sleep on the floor. I'll do anything it takes, but it makes me miserable to feel him slipping away every night when the answer could be within our reach.

However, talking to him may come sooner than I planned. I get downstairs to find both men waiting for me in the kitchen, which is *not* normal.

"I made breakfast," Ben says, pulling out a chair for me and presenting me with a mug of coffee and then a plate of irresistible farm food. Fried mushrooms, eggs, and bacon, with a thick slab of toast, butter melting on top.

"Thanks!" I take the plate, and I'm about to demolish the toast when I notice them looking at me.

I've never liked being watched while I'm eating. It makes me immediately and terribly self-conscious, as if I'm doing something wrong by it. As if I should have refused the food or asked for raw kale and sunflower seeds instead.

But there's nothing about Caleb or Ben that looks anything other than their normal handsome and slightly-obsessed-with-me selves right now. Caleb has his usual bearded grin as he sits next to me, and Ben his usual hungry gaze as he sits on the other side.

Relax, Ireland. They aren't Brian and your sister. They're not judging you.

It's still hard to take that first bite, but Ben's look of masculine pride as I moan around his meal is worth it. They love to take care of me—I'm in danger of being downright spoiled. They wash my hair in the shower, they launder my clothes, and they pack my bags. They plug my phone and laptop into chargers if I forget to at night, and they put jars and vases full of fresh sunflowers in every room simply because they know sunflowers make me smile. They give me the second-best spot on the couch—Greta-dog gets the first-best—and then, of course, there are the hours and hours of mind-blowing sex.

So it's not unusual for them to pamper me with a delicious meal, but it is unusual for them not to be working right now. For them to be here watching me eat instead of out in the fields or in town, or even working on restoring the tavern now that some of the insurance money has trickled in.

I glance between them, wondering if I should stop eating.

"Move in with us," Caleb blurts out, and Ben groans.

"We were going to wait until after she ate," he says irritably. "Remember?"

I swallow and look at them both. They are deadly earnest, sitting on the literal edges of their seats with green and brown eyes trained on me.

"You aren't serious," I say weakly.

"We've never been more serious about anything," Ben says after giving Caleb a *let-me-handle-this* look. "We're in love with you."

My mouth drops open.

Caleb laughs. "Peach, it can't be that much of a surprise. We can't keep our hands off you, we call you constantly when you're away, and we never let you out of our sight when you're here. Of course we're in love with you."

"I just—I—" I'm stammering and also trying to keep my chin from quivering. "No one's ever said that to me before."

Both boys blink at me with such sweet surprise that I have to rub at my nose to fight off the sudden about-to-cry sting there. And then before I can do or say anything else, I'm being yanked into a fierce embrace between the two of them, and even on their knees around me they're still tall enough that I feel completely surrounded.

I bury my face into Caleb's neck, rubbing against his soft beard.

"We've been in love since the moment we met you," he says softly.

Ben is moving my hair aside to kiss the nape of my neck with firm, warm lips.

"We've known you were ours since day one," Caleb continues. "Please say yes, Ireland. Please say you love us back. Move in with us."

My heart's so full it feels like it will burst.

How can this be real? How can this be true?

And how is it that I've never wanted anything as much as to be with these two men for the rest of forever?

"I love you back," I mumble against Caleb's skin. "I think I've been in love with the both of you since the first day too."

I'm rewarded for this admission, squeezed and kissed and loved on. Petted and stroked until I feel all spoiled again.

"You haven't answered us about moving in," Ben says. "Why? Is it work? Family?"

I can work remotely, and I would probably pay money to not see my sister, so it's not either of those things. But I'm not really sure what it *is* either. Some kind of lingering insecurity, maybe? This stubborn doubt that I don't really belong with them because of my body?

I hate these gross thoughts. I banish them to the back of

my mind and try to focus on what I know instead—Caleb and Ben love me and I love them, and there's no practical reason keeping me from moving in other than that it's fast and this relationship is still so new. Well, that and one person in our bed can't seem to stay there for the whole night.

Maybe this is my chance to be brave...and to nudge Ben into bravery along with me.

"I'll say yes," I decide, "if Ben can sleep the whole night with us."

Behind me, Ben's body goes still and stonelike. "Pardon?" he asks, as if he didn't hear correctly.

"I think you heard me," I reply gently. "If we can find a way for you to sleep through the night with us, I'll move in."

CHAPTER SIXTEEN

BEN

Ireland is looking at me over her shoulder, her blue eyes clear and serious, and Caleb's looking at me the same way. All concern and desire. It makes my chest tighten, and I stand up to get some space while I think.

"I didn't think anyone cared much one way or the other," I say, going over to the counter and bracing my hands against it. I take a few deep breaths, trying to organize my thoughts, which are currently in a defensive swirl. "It's not like we fuck any less because I sleep alone."

"It's not about fucking," Ireland says, and I hear her stand up and walk over to me. She slides her hands around my waist and leans her head against my back, molding her curves to me.

It feels so good. Good enough that I realize how tense my body is, as if I'm fortifying myself against some kind of danger.

I inhale, forcing myself to remember that I'm *here*, not in Marjah listening to the sporadic crackle of bullets and the distant thuds of mortar shells. I'm here at the farm with the two people I love. Two people I'm trying to love better than I have been.

"I have trouble sleeping," I admit, and even that admission

is harder than it should be. I don't know why, when Ireland's arguably seen the worst of my baggage already, but I can't stand that I'm not able to do something as normal as sleep with the people I love—or hell, sleep properly at all. It makes me feel juvenile and antisocial and abnormal, and I hate it.

But Ireland deserves the truth, and I made promises to her that I plan on keeping.

I take a deep breath and keep going. "It's hard to get to sleep, and I have nightmares when I do. Bad nightmares that leave me sweaty and thrashing and kicking. The TV and lights help sometimes but not always. I *want* to sleep with you two— God, I want to so much—but I'm terrified of hurting you while I'm dreaming—and on top of that, it's not fair to make your sleep worse just so I can share a bed with you. You deserve rest."

"And you don't?" Ireland murmurs.

I make an impatient noise. "Not if it makes it *harder* for you to sleep!"

"I can handle myself," she says stubbornly.

"Me too," says a deep voice next to me. I look up into the soft-green eyes of my best friend and lover.

"It's not that easy," I say. "*I* don't even like being around myself at night. I would never ask someone else to be."

"But you're not asking. We are." Ireland squeezes me tighter and then slips under my arm so she can peer up into my face. "Please, Ben? Can we try it?"

What man on earth could resist these hopeful big blue eyes? This soft, pouting mouth? I'm nothing but weakness when it comes to her, and I think she knows it because her pleading expression starts looking more and more triumphant the longer we stare at each other.

Finally I heave a giant breath. "Okay," I agree, and I know I sound reluctant as fuck—because I am. "We'll try tonight. And then you'll move in with us."

The firmness in my words leaves no room for argument, and it sounds more like a military command than a boyfriend asking someone he loves to share his life. But I don't care. I don't care at all because she gives me a sweet smile and an even sweeter "Yes, Ben."

And then breakfast is left to cool on the table as we yank each other upstairs to fuck in the bed we'll all share tonight.

◆ ◆ ◆ ◆

The thought of tonight haunts me as I toil over the new floors in the tavern this afternoon. As I work, my mind fills with worrisome scenarios ranging from good-old-fashioned insomnia to the humiliating release of tears I sometimes wake to find on my face.

It's not a big deal. It's not a big deal, I repeat to myself as I work on fitting and gluing the floorboards down. People sleep with their lovers all the time, and surely I'm not the only person in the history of human relationships to have trouble sleeping. *Ireland and Caleb love me,* I remind myself and feel the tight anxiety in my chest loosen a little.

I want to make them happy. I want to be closer to them.

I can do this.

I've survived years of bullying in school, and I've survived war zones that have since become legendary for how hellish they were. Fists and bullets and fire—I've lived through it all.

I can survive the night snuggled against someone I love.

The tavern door opens, letting in a welcome rectangle of warm sunlight and fresh air, and I look up to see Ireland in the doorway wearing the short skirt Caleb and I beg her to wear all the time and a blouse thing tied around her waist, showing off a tempting tease of pale skin. With her blue lipstick and colorful clothes, she's like kissable, lickable city-girl candy, and I want to wrap my fist in all that dark, silky hair and press my mouth against all her sugar. My cock is pulsing to life just looking at her.

I wipe the sweat from my brow with my forearm and get to my feet, taking off my work gloves so I can grab at her and kiss her. She giggles as I do, fussing about her lipstick and halfheartedly trying to keep her distance from my sweaty, sawdusted body, but she eventually gives in, letting me crowd her against the wall until she's moaning into my mouth and arching her soft breasts into my hands.

The door opens again and Caleb walks in. "Oh fuck, you guys," he says in a husky voice. "Fuck yeah."

"No, no, no," Ireland protests as Caleb joins us and starts in on her neck. "We just fucked this morning. Twice!"

"Doesn't matter," I mumble, brushing my thumbs across her hard, needy nipples. My cock is raging to be inside her, and with her short, flirty skirt, it's all too easy to push my hand between her legs to find out if she's wet enough to fuck.

She is.

She moans again as I slide my thumb under her panties and start rolling it against her stiff little clit.

Caleb's already grinding his erection against her hip, taking up where I left off on teasing her nipples, and I whisper in her ear, "We could do it a third time...and a fourth time...and a fifth time...right here against this wall. You coming so hard on our cocks that you can't even hold yourself up..."

Her eyes are fluttering almost all the way closed, and for a minute, I think she's going to agree, but then her phone buzzes in her skirt pocket and she jolts.

"You guys," she admonishes, pushing us back with a flat palm to each of our chests. "I'm supposed to meet a reporter from the *Star* at any minute, and I can't do that with lipstick all over my face and a used condom in my pocket."

"Well, obviously we'd throw the condom away after—"

Her hand moves from my chest to my mouth. "Your talking privileges are suspended for the time being." Her half smile fades a little. "It's important to me, Ben. My pictures of Holm and all the rebuilding that's been happening here could be the start of something exciting, and I don't want to fuck it up. Now where can I fix my lipstick?"

Caleb points her to the bathroom—which has running water and a mirror, even if it's still trashed from the storm—and then turns back to me with a thoughtful expression. "You think we should go with her to meet this reporter? Like emotional support?"

I'm already walking toward the bag I've got sitting on a makeshift table made out of sawhorses and plywood. I rummage for a clean shirt and wipe the sweat and blue lipstick off my face. I'm thinking of her anxious, hopeful expression just now, and also about the way she's been all over this town taking pictures of both the tragic and the hopeful.

I wonder again why she isn't already doing something she obviously loves so much.

"Yeah. I think we should."

♦ ♦ ♦ ♦

The reporter and her accompanying photographer are friendly and engaging. The reporter interviews Ireland for a good forty-five minutes as we stroll around the recovering but still visibly scarred Main Street while the photographer drifts away and back again to take pictures of various buildings and piles of construction materials. Caleb and I more or less hang back, and I'm sure we look like country boy versions of bodyguards as we trail behind our girl and cast looming six-foot-plus shadows along the street. The photographer seems a little nervous around us, but the reporter is just curious, peeking back over her shoulder and then back at Ireland, as if trying to guess if we're related or something. It's strangely irritating, but I force myself to remember that two is not the usual number of boyfriends to have. And also that Ireland wants to impress this person, so it won't do her any good if I spend the rest of the afternoon scowling.

Ireland herself is adorably oblivious to our presence as we go, so used to us following her around like overgrown—and overprotective—puppies that she only spares us a glance every now and then. But each glance is elated and grateful and makes me fall in love with her all over again.

"Well," the reporter says, hitting *stop* on her phone's recording app and giving Ireland a warm smile, "I think that's probably all I need. We'll just get some photos of you and then head on out."

Ireland freezes, and I can see the moment the panic hits her like a lightning bolt. She swallows, and there seems to be effort in keeping her voice light when she says, "Photos of me?"

"Of course!" the reporter chirps. "I think it will really drive home the point of the piece, which is all about the girl behind the camera, you know? The face behind the pictures that everyone's been talking about."

It's astonishing how fast the well-kissed, confident, animated woman taking them around the town vanishes. In her place is a woman who looks terrified, tugging unconsciously at her hemline and rounding her shoulders ever so slightly, as if she's trying to hunch into herself.

As if she's trying to hide.

I don't understand it, but every protective instinct in me roars to life, and they must be in Caleb too because he's already taking a step forward, as if to put himself between Ireland and danger. Danger in this case being a chirpy, five-foot-four reporter.

I step forward too and put my hand against Ireland's back.

"Do you want your...friends...in the picture?" the reporter asks, looking at us with avid interest.

"Boyfriends," I correct automatically and then realize I've made a mistake. Ireland stiffens against my hand at the same time as the reporter's eyes gleam with unmistakable delight. I can practically see her brain whirring with ways to work this juicy tidbit into the story.

Shit.

"Boyfriends?" she repeats and gives us the *oh cool, uh-huh, uh-huh, I'm pretending to think this is totally normal* nod and smile. "And you met after the storm?"

I can feel the deep breath Ireland takes. "Actually, no," she answers, and she answers with a lifted chin and the confident, cheerful smile I've come to know and love. "We met before the tornado." And she gives a charming and PG-rated account of how we all came to know each other and how the storm brought us together.

The reporter can't hide her excitement. "This is such a cute story," she gushes. "Can I make it part of the feature? I mean, with a picture of the three of you..."

I'm about to say no on Ireland's behalf. It's clear there's something about being in a picture that makes her uncomfortable, and I won't have anything making her unhappy, but she beats me to an answer.

"Yes," she says, and while I can sense her bravery, I can also sense her pride. "You can put it in the article, with a picture of the three of us."

And when Caleb and I arrange ourselves around her, our arms crossing behind her back to wrap around her waist, it feels like the most natural thing in the world. Not just the holding of her between us, which isn't new, but doing it publicly.

I give her a kiss on the head between flashes of the camera.

"I love you," I tell her.

"I'm real proud for the world to know I'm your boyfriend," Caleb adds quietly.

Ireland flushes a happy flush, and her smile for the camera goes brighter.

"Okay, I think we've got it," the reporter says cheerfully after the photographer gives her a nod. "I'm going to work fast—we're hoping to get this up by late evening!"

It's enough to send another nervous look flitting across Ireland's face, but the reporter and photographer are quick with their goodbyes, and there's no chance for Ireland to change her mind about anything. When they leave, she turns back to us, chewing on her blue lower lip. "Do you think I did okay? Did I talk enough about the rebuilding and the storm? And the picture—"

"You did great, peach," Caleb says, wrapping his big hands around her shoulders and dropping a kiss onto her hair. "You did perfect."

She sighs like she doesn't believe him but isn't willing to argue and turns back to the tavern. We follow, stepping onto the sidewalk right as Mrs. Parry's nephew walks past with a bucket of paint in each hand, headed for the little volunteer library next to the tavern. I give him a nod, although something about the way the older man eyes Ireland has me pressing my hand more firmly against her back, those protective instincts still rearing strong.

Ireland, probably still chewing over the interview in her mind, doesn't notice Lyle Parry or my reaction to him. I shoot a glance at Caleb, who also takes note of the smirking way Lyle is staring at Ireland, and Caleb understands immediately. He hangs back, ostensibly to talk to Lyle, but really to step between Lyle and Ireland while I shepherd her back inside the tavern.

Caleb and Lyle greet each other and make some small talk as we all move down the sidewalk, and it's with some relief when I get to the door of the tavern and push it open. Ireland is walking inside as Lyle lowers his voice and mutters to Caleb, "She must be something else in bed, huh?"

"Excuse me?" Caleb asks coldly.

"You know what I'm talking about," Lyle says in a winky-nudgy kind of tone, which is still loud enough to carry easily through the threshold of the open tavern door. I try to shut it, but I'm not quick enough. Lyle's stupid voice still reaches us. "The chunky ones are always better in the sack. More grateful, you see? Makes them try harder."

Next to me, Ireland goes completely still, and I'm torn between the need to comfort her and shield her from every shitty thing in this world and my rage. I want to go out there and beat the teeth out of Lyle Parry's head. I want to wring him like a towel and hang him up to dry.

But one look at Ireland's face reminds me what my priorities are.

I gather her into my arms and hold her to my chest. "Fuck him," I murmur.

Caleb outside growls, "You'll talk about Ireland with some fucking respect, Lyle, or face the consequences." And then Caleb storms inside amid Lyle's shocked sputters, slamming the tavern door shut behind him.

"God, Ireland, I'm so fucking sorry he said that," Caleb says with misery painted all over his expression. He comes to stand next to us, putting his hand on Ireland's shoulder, but she shakes her head and takes a step away from us.

"It's fine," she says in a falsely bright voice. "I've been one of the 'chunky ones' for a long time. I'm used to it."

Everything about her is armored right now—her forced smile and her tense stance—and when I reach for her again, she moves out of range.

"Ireland," I say, and my voice is lower and sharper than I want it to be, but seeing her upset like this has me on edge. "He's a fucking idiot. You're beautiful and perfect."

If my words were arrows, they'd be bouncing hopelessly off her armor now and dropping uselessly to the floor.

"Of course I am," she says with more of that false, hard brightness. "I know that. Well, I think I'm going to head back to the farmhouse now—I should probably get some work done before dinner, and I thought I could make dinner tonight since you guys usually make it, so I should also head out to the store..."

She's babbling, talking fast and lively, as if worried that if she doesn't, we'll try to comfort her again. She gets her things, and I grab my things too, deciding to call it a day at the tavern. I don't want to be apart from her even in the best of situations, but especially not when some shitbag has said something awful about her.

We all head outside together, Ireland still chattering until the moment we get into separate cars and drive home. And once we're in the kitchen—Caleb and I taking over dinner preparation by unspoken agreement—with her working at the table, Caleb tries to bring it up once again.

"I don't like that he said those things," he says while stabbing his fingers through his hair. "I hate even more that they've upset you. Tell me how to fix it, peach. Tell me how to make you feel better."

She looks up from her laptop, and when she does, her eyes are hard and her mouth is set in a mulish line. "You can make me feel better by not talking about it."

Caleb opens his mouth, and she holds up a hand. "I mean it, Carpenter." Her voice is truly serious, absent any fake cheeriness or falsely casual confidence now. "I don't want to talk about this."

A limit is a limit is a limit. An entire adult lifetime of polyamory has taught us that. Caleb gives me a helpless look, and I give him a small nod, telling him I understand his frustration, his need to protect our woman from any and all pain, but also that we can't do that if she doesn't want us to. And hell, maybe it would be impossible anyway, because I'm not sure *how* to comfort her. How can she not see how fucking beautiful she is? How devastatingly sexy that body is? How much we want to love and cherish it and her?

We make dinner, and then we make love, shower, and make love again. As I watch her pretend her way through a normal evening, I see the waves of hurt and anger flicker through her like electric currents. I see her swing between the unfocused and unconscious real confidence I've grown used to from her and the almost-harsh forced confidence she had in the tavern after we heard Lyle. I see her move from happy and sexy to insecure and worried and then back to happy and sexy again.

And I realize something about myself as I watch her. Something not even years of therapy could teach me— something that seems painfully obvious now that I see it.

People aren't just one thing.

People aren't just confident and then that's it, there's nothing that can dent that confidence. People aren't just brave and then free from fear their entire lives. We exist in tangles of virtue and weakness simultaneously—we are the best and worst of ourselves all at the same time.

A soldier who faced bullets and bombs but is now afraid of the dark.

A scared, sensitive boy who made himself so tough he's forgotten how to be vulnerable.

A man who is fierce possession and cold reserve all at once.

And maybe all that is okay—maybe words like *best* and *worst* or *virtue* and *weakness* are misleading. Maybe they incorrectly assign value to things that aren't good or bad in and of themselves; they're simply *human*.

And it's with this epiphany that I climb into bed with the people I love. I wrap my arms around Ireland, one of my hands finding Caleb's and lacing with his fingers, and I close my eyes against the darkness. For the first time, I don't fight the fear. I don't struggle with it. I allow it just to *be*, bobbing on the surface of my mind along with all the other things I'm thinking and feeling. Like that I love Ireland and Caleb, that I want this to be for the rest of our lives, that I want them inside every wall or gate I've ever erected. That Greta-dog is almost out of dog treats, and that once I get the next insurance check, I should be able to order stuff for the new tavern kitchen.

That actually it's okay to be afraid, okay to be anxious, and it would be okay no matter what, but it's especially okay with the woman I love nestled against my chest and the man I love snoring gently beside her.

Somehow, by some magic, as I trace the oval glow and shadow of the nightlight on the ceiling, I manage to fall asleep.

And I sleep the whole night through.

CHAPTER SEVENTEEN

IRELAND

He did it.

I wake up wrapped in the world's warmest, best-smelling blanket, and when I open my eyes to see Ben's face all open and young-looking as he sleeps, a spike of joy goes right through my chest.

He did it.

He did it for me—for all of us—and suddenly, with a crest of dizzying happiness, I can see the future ahead for the three of us. Me moving in, us sharing sex and sleep every night. Maybe someday we could share even more...weddings and babies and all the things everyone else gets to have. Why not us? It may look different, it may take figuring out, but to share forever and more with these men would be worth it. So fucking worth it.

I slide out of bed and take a quick shower as they doze on. Dawn is breaking and they'll be up soon, and I want to have a big breakfast waiting when they are. I'm already smiling to myself as I imagine giving them the news. I'll tell them I'm going to move in, and then they'll grin—even my broody soldier will be smiling—and then they'll start thanking me with their mouths and their fingers and their cocks...

With a full-body shiver of anticipation, I grab my phone to go downstairs and the screen goes bright. Notification after notification are stacked—some from social media, some from email—but what strikes me first is a text from my boss, looking like it came in right after my three-hour fuckfest with Ben and Caleb began last night.

> *Great interview! We've already had two*
> *potential clients contact Typeset wanting*
> *your photography as part of a campaign!!!!*

So the interview did go live last night...and presumably the picture along with it. But before I can properly process my panic, I see a text from a contact I should have deleted a long time ago: Brian.

> *Still look like a cow. Guess you're a slut now too.*

I nearly drop the phone.

Oh God, oh God, oh God.

I look over at Ben and Caleb—both of them still stretched and sprawled like teenage boys across the bed—and for one painfully acute moment, I want to wake them up. I want them to pull me back into bed, where it's warm and cozy and where I'm loved without reserve. I know if I tell them what Brian said, they'll be furious. They'll scowl and make angry bear noises and threaten to kill him. And then they'll fuck me with all that pent-up anger—not directed at me but *for* me—anger stemming from the need to protect me. And I'll feel better.

Except maybe I won't. Not until I figure out exactly

what's going on, at least.

And maybe, a cold, slimy voice whispers, *they wouldn't do that at all. Maybe after what Lyle said yesterday, they'll start to realize you're not worth protecting. You're not worth the effort. Why would you be? It's not like there are men lining up to take their place.*

"Shut up," I whisper back to the voice. "Shut up, shut up, shut up."

But it doesn't shut up as I creep down the stairs in the near-dawn darkness. The voice keeps going. And the longer it talks, the more sense it starts to make. Especially as I open up my laptop at the kitchen table and see an email from the reporter in my inbox, with the subject line *Here it is!!!*

I open the email and click the link.

I immediately wish I hadn't.

The picture of me with Caleb and Ben is at the very top, and right away I can see it's not a flattering picture. The skirt I bought in a fit of bravery after breaking up with Brian—the same skirt Caleb and Ben beg me to wear all the time—does nothing to hide thighs that are too wide and too pale and too dimpled. My cropped blouse that felt so cute when Caleb kept trying to yank it off me so he could nuzzle my breasts looks embarrassingly small now. The little strip of belly that seemed spunky and adorable looks sad and not a little oblivious on the screen. Even the long wavy hair and colorful lipstick—a look I'm normally so proud of, a look I've shown off on Instagram more times than I can count—seem pathetically desperate. When I went into town that day, I felt bold and sexy and fun, but looking at the picture now, it's like every single element that makes Ireland Mills interesting or pretty or *anything* has been flattened into an image that screams *trying too hard.*

Not for the first time, I wish I weren't so goddamned short. I wish I were five foot nine or ten, like the famous plus-size models on the covers of magazines, and not five foot two. I wish my curves were spread out instead of all squished together, I wish I carried my weight differently.

The cold, slimy voice chants wishes along with me— wishes that pass through my mind in less than a minute but get darker and darker as they go. I wish my breasts were smaller. I wish my belly were too. I wish I looked thin...I wish I *were* thin. I wish I were born that way.

I wish I wasn't born at all.

A pulse of jagged, ruthless satisfaction follows the thought; it's like pressing down on a bruise.

It's starkly comforting to acknowledge the truth at last.

I wish I wasn't born at all, not into this body. I hate this body.

I run my hands through my hair, tugging at it. How can this be me thinking these thoughts? Me, who just a month ago was a newly confident woman with tons of body-positive bloggers in her Instagram feed and a wardrobe full of clothes she actually wanted to wear? I thought I was over feeling bad about my body, that I'd solved my insecurity, and all it takes is one picture to make me wish I'd never been born? How weak am I?

Desperate for any new input to shake me away from my thoughts, I look back at the picture. The boys look amazing, of course, even though they'd both been working outside and sweating that day. They look like models for some kind of country boy calendar, T-shirts clinging to tight stomachs and belted jeans showing off narrow hips and distinct bulges behind their zippers. They look like the epitome of alpha males, like they should have a willowy, all-American blonde between them, not a dumpy brunette who looks like an art school dropout.

Although I'm not *even* an art school dropout. I'm something much worse: a girl who was too chicken even to go in the first place.

The caption for the picture is journalistically spare:

Mills, 24, and her two boyfriends,
Caleb Carpenter, 33, and Ben Weber, 33, both of Holm, Kansas.
They met the weekend of the tornado.

The article itself is fantastic—I can recognize that in a distant part of my brain. The reporter paints a picture of me as smart and vibrant and creative, all of my quotes sound insightful and intelligent, and all the photographs of mine they feature are strikingly composed and emotional.

But I of all people know it doesn't matter how smart I am, or how talented. When you're fat, all of those qualities are erased. All that exists to represent you as a three-dimensional and nuanced human is your fatness, and your fatness is translated in a kind of visual shorthand for all sorts of moral failings. Laziness. Gluttony. Uncleanliness. An unholy lack of self-control and self-discipline.

The very sight of you is almost like an affront; your existence is almost offensive.

I could have invented CRISPR or fed thousands in the streets of Calcutta and it wouldn't have mattered so long as my picture was at the top of the article. It's why I've hidden behind the camera for so long—because to be in front of the lens is to acknowledge that I exist in this body. To be smiling is to not participate in the expectation that I should be ashamed.

I should close the tab. I should, I should, but the rational part of me is gone, cowering and crying somewhere, and all that's left is the part of me that can't resist pressing on the bruise some more.

Which is why I scroll down to the comments section.

It's a mistake.

Even the awful part of me that whispers about how much I hate my own body sees that it's a mistake, because it turns out that even the worst cruelty I can muster toward myself is nothing compared to what strangers can say on the internet.

Why are *they* with *her*? one anonymous commenter says. *Two hot guys with an overweight girl just doesn't add up.*

Another anonymous commenter adds below, *I bet there's not even room in the bed for all of them.*

Why is the Star *glorifying this unnatural sex cult?* SoonerInTheKitchen replies. *This is clearly a relationship built on sin.*

xfitwarrior says, *Shame on this paper for promoting disease and glorifying overweight ppl when being overweight is the number one cause of death in America and costs billions of dollars to taxpayers every year. Obesity IS UNHEALTHY. Obesity KILLS. Shame on you!*

A reply to that comment by ketogoddess87 says, *You don't*

know where she is in her journey! She might have already lost a hundred pounds and be on the way to getting healthier! You can't judge someone's health by just one picture!

QueenSizeGirlsDoItBetter replies to that comment, saying, *Wherever she is on her journey, she shouldn't be wearing clothes like that. I'm a plus sized girl myself, and even I know that nobody wants to see allllll that body hanging out everywhere!*

I guess there's no accounting for taste, KSUBetcha says. *'Caleb' and 'Ben' here prove that. Chubby chasing much?*

CalebAndBenLovePiggies replies to that comment with *oink oink.*

My fingers are trembling as I scroll down, but I can't stop myself, can't look away. It's some kind of sick impulse, forcing me to read every nasty comment, every judgmental observation about my size, every reply that seems well-intentioned but is actually still incredibly hurtful.

I can't breathe. I can't think. At some point, my brain begins sending out panic hormones, flooding my veins with the need to run, to fight, to scream.

Danger, my nervous system blares at me. *Danger.*

It doesn't matter that it's "just" the internet, that I can't see the faces or hear the voices of the people who've written these things, because it's still real. Real people still said these things in a place where I, a real person, could see them. Where I could see myself talked about with—at best—condescension, and—at worst—hostile disgust.

This is what you get, the awful voice whispers. *For thinking you could have more. Wanting to be a famous photographer. Dating two men way out of your league.*

The voice is right. I was stupid and foolish to ever believe otherwise.

And I'm not really sure what to do with that epiphany, or with the nauseous, panicked urges roiling through me, until I see the last comment and feel like my heart is going to explode from beating so fast.

An anonymous commenter has posted a link to Ben's tavern on Yelp, and when I follow the link, I see the page has been spammed with one-star reviews. They're predictably pointless and crude—mostly rehashing the same kinds of awful things said in the comments section of the article—but they hurt me in an entirely new place. It's one thing to be insulted and dehumanized, to have my potential photography career burned down before my eyes. Those things stab at places that have been stabbed at before.

But to have Ben and Caleb insulted and dehumanized— and to have Ben's livelihood threatened—all for the sin of loving me, well...

There's no scar tissue there. It's a fresh, new, terrifying pain.

I was reluctant to allow that photo for a few reasons. Because I wasn't mentally ready for it. Because I've spent the last ten or so years defining myself as the person *behind* the camera except for carefully angled and curated social media pictures. Because I was nervous about publicly declaring myself in a poly relationship.

Never, ever, not once, had it occurred to me the picture would hurt Ben and Caleb. I never once considered the cost they would pay to love me and my body.

God. What have I done?

I'm about to close out of everything—a survival mechanism, really, not out of some admirable display of willpower—when my phone chimes again, an innocent little *pling* of a text message. Except it's from Brian again. And it's actually a voice message this time.

I know, on an instinctual level, that I shouldn't play it. I know that nothing good can come of it, that there's nothing helpful or insightful that he can say to me. But I'm too broken down not to crave that last strike, one last wound, and my hand is moving over the phone before I can stop myself. I hit play.

"You know"—Brian's voice comes over the speaker, loud and brittle and mean—"if you wanted more than one dick, I could have paid a friend to fuck you. I would've had to pay him a *lot*, though."

He's drunk. I can tell by the wobble of his voice, a wobble I heard frequently enough, although never at—I check the clock above the stove—six thirty in the morning.

"I kept wondering," he rambles on, "how the fuck dare *you* break up with *me*? Me, when I was being so fucking nice to you in the first place? And now I know why—it's because you're a whore. And I don't know what you did to make those men pretend to like you, but I know for a fact they're just pretending." A hiccup. "And I'm going to prove it. I found your boyfriend's little tavern, and I posted it on that bullshit article, and I'm going to tell everyone what a fucking pervert he is— him and his fucking farmer friend. We'll see if they're willing to be nice to you after you've ruined their lives."

The message ends, and with it, the last, tiny thread of

self-control I'd been clinging to. I shouldn't be surprised at his hateful words, that he's the one who outed Ben's tavern on the article. And yet, I am. I'm exhausted by it, by the relentlessness of having a body that's such an easy target, by the cultural certainty that anyone who loves me or my body is some kind of deviant freak. That anyone who cares for me deserves to be punished, and I do too, for not staying where we're supposed to—in the neatly cruel categories the rest of the world decides.

I press my face into my hands, tears running out of my eyes like water dribbles from a tap—steadily and without effort. It barely even feels like I'm crying. It barely feels like anything, as if my body has put the act of crying on autopilot as my mind races through the implications of this.

I've been stupid.

I've been selfish.

I thought people like Lyle Parry were the exception. I thought the little cocoon of sex and domesticity we spun here at the farm could last forever. But I forgot the rules, forgot the lessons that all those cheesy romantic movies had taught me.

There is no forever for girls like me. There is no happily ever after for a curvy girl, and if I try to force it, I'll only end up hurting Ben and Caleb more. I'll only end up wrecking their lives. The town will scorn them, just like Lyle did. Ben's tavern business will wither under the scorch of online mockery, and gentle, sweet Caleb will be torn up from the inside out with every cruel comment that comes our way.

No, this was doomed to fail from the start, and I'm so ashamed it took this long for me to figure it out. I feel greedy and grasping and worse—I feel naïve.

So fucking naïve.

With a swallowed sob, I slam the laptop shut.

I know what I have to do. It's awful and scary and I already hate myself for it, but I'll hate myself more if I stay, knowing what it will cost Ben and Caleb to love me.

I stand up, wipe the tears from my face, and turn to go upstairs.

And find both men standing in the doorway to the kitchen, watching me with clenched fists and heaving chests.

"Was that him?" Ben asks quietly. "Your ex?"

I don't even know what to say or what to do, because the humiliation of them hearing Brian's message blocks every neuron in my brain and every nerve ending in my body. I am living humiliation. I am shame and anger embodied.

I am shaking.

"I'll kill him," my normally sweet Caleb vows, his jaw tight under his beard, and something in my chest snaps in half. Gentle Caleb all murderous and Ben looking like a cold, clinical soldier instead of the complicated, sensitive man I know him actually to be—it's too much. This is breaking them in every possible way. It's breaking me too, and it has to stop.

"No one talks to you like that," Caleb seethes, every cord in his neck and forearms standing out. "Fucking no one. We're going to take care of it, peach, trust me."

Ben's gaze is astute, piercing, when it locks on my face. "Don't believe a word of it," he orders. "Not a single word of it. He's bitter, and bitter people will do anything to make someone else feel as shitty as they do."

"And he's an asshole," Caleb adds.

"And he's an asshole," Ben concedes, his eyes still pinned

on me. "He can't hurt us, and we won't let him hurt you. Got it?"

But can't they see that I'm already hurting? That they will be hurting too? All because we forgot the rules?

"I'm going," I say. "I'm going back to Kansas City."

Caleb's eyes flare green with panic. "No, peach. Don't say that."

"I can't do this!" The words are ripped out of me, right from the gut. I'm crying again. "I can't do this with you two."

They flinch at that, and I use their momentary surprise to push past them and go upstairs, throwing all my stuff into my bag once I get there. The toothbrush knocking cutely against theirs on the bathroom counter. The salon shampoo and conditioner perched on the shower ledge. All the lacy, sexy things I bought to please them...and all the lacy, sexy things they bought for me. All the clothes and half-read paperbacks and charging cords and other evidence that I'd been slowly moving in all this time.

It all gets packed up, and when I get downstairs, Caleb and Ben are sitting on the sofa by the front door—Caleb with his head in his hands and Ben in the deliberate pose of a hawk visually tracking prey.

I need to walk to the door now. I need to go. And yet I can't make my feet move. Can't force myself to admit this is the end.

"Don't do this," Ben says. The sharp cuts of his cheekbones are flooded with color, and in his utter and perfect stillness, the corners of his sensual mouth have gone white. "Don't let him win."

"It's not just him," I say. "It's everyone. Everything."

"But it's not everyone," Caleb whispers, looking up at me. "Because the three of us know the truth. That we're in love and nothing will change that."

Sweet Caleb. "It's easy to say that now," I tell them. "But it won't be for long."

"Ireland," Ben says, and that's all he needs to say. He packs every feeling, every question, and every plea into those three syllables. I promise myself I'll hold on to the sound of him saying my name forever.

"It was beautiful, loving you," I say to them both. "I wish it could have lasted."

"No." They say it at the same time, and I take a breath.

"I'm the one saying *no* now," I tell them. "This is my limit. I finally found it." I try bravely to crack a smile. "Goodbye. And please don't follow me, I have to do this. For all of us."

I finally make myself take those steps across the room, past two wonderful men who deserve better. And then I walk out the door and out of their lives.

CHAPTER EIGHTEEN

IRELAND

Two Weeks Later

"Ireland, there's someone here to see you."

I look up from my desk to see Drew standing next to it, looking mildly uncomfortable. My heart seizes at the same time as my stomach clenches. "Is it Caleb?" I whisper, hoping for it to be and also dreading it at the same time. It's been two weeks since I left the farm, two weeks of nonstop calls and texts and voicemails from my boys. Caleb's resorted to trying to get a message to me through Drew.

And Ben...he's mailed me letters. In his heart-wrenchingly precise print, he begs me to come home, tells me he loves me over and over again, will sleep the whole night through with me every night for the rest of our lives...

I've broken their hearts by leaving, but what could I have done? What could I have said? *I have objective proof that I'll ruin your lives if I let you love me? The world will never accept that you love me and my body....and I don't know that I can accept it either?*

They would have tried to talk me out of these conclusions, they would have fought for me to stay, and I wouldn't have been able to bear it. I would have caved and stayed and then hated myself for my weakness as the months dragged on and their lives became worse and worse.

No, this was for their own good, and my own good as well. I needed a harsh dose of reality.

That doesn't make it any easier, though. Drew has found me crying in the break room more than once, and I've fallen asleep at night only by drinking way too many vodka lemonades and sleeping on the couch.

It's too hard to sleep alone in a bed now that I know what it feels like to sleep tangled and warm with two other people.

But I did the right thing. Of that, I'm certain.

So I push away my disappointment when Drew shakes his head. "No, it's a woman. But Caleb did call again this morning. Are you sure you can't—?"

"I'm sure," I interrupt, the lie stinging my lips as it comes out. "As sure as sure can be."

♦ ♦ ♦ ♦

Typeset is a very typical kind of marketing office—it's almost insufferably trendy, with exposed brick and an open workroom with rows of shared desks. Only the meeting rooms provide any modicum of privacy, and even then the privacy is fairly notional, given the walls and doors are made of glass.

This is where I meet my visitor, a young woman standing by the window looking out over the skyline. She's wearing jeans and a tight T-shirt, so she's not the typical Typeset client or the kind of young professional who haunts this part of the city. She turns to face me, and I realize two things at once.

First, she's got the kind of body I long to have. Small breasts, model height, the majority of her weight around her hips and in her thighs. Pear-shaped, but the sexiest fucking pear in the world. Even though she probably weighs as much as me or more, she looks like she belongs in a catalog or on a runway, whereas I look like an extra bar wench on a medieval film set.

The second thing I realize is that she's also staggeringly beautiful. No makeup. Simple clothes. She's flawlessly skinned and glowing, gorgeous without all the things I use as a mask—the lipsticks and the bright colors. She's effortless and easy and perfect. Damn her.

"Hello," she says, picking a chair and sitting down, as if this is her meeting room and not mine. "You Ireland?"

"Um, yes," I say. "I'm sorry, have we—?"

She waves a hand. "No, but why would we have? I'm Mackenna."

"Okay..." I say hesitantly, feeling like I should be able to infer more from her name than I am.

"Caleb and Ben's ex-girlfriend," she supplies.

"Oh," I say, surprised, and then, "*Oh*," as I realize I have no idea why she's here, but it can't be good. "Look," I say, trying to head off any ex drama at the pass, "we're actually not together anymore—"

Another hand wave. She's got the Deathly Hallows symbol tattooed on her wrist and an old-fashioned *Mom* tattoo splashing across her upper arm. She has gold-brown skin, coffee-colored eyes that gleam in the hot sunlight coming in through the window, and glossy, thick hair that looks so good I want to bite my knuckle in jealousy.

Impatient. That's what Caleb had said about her, and as I look at her now, I can see it. In the way she shakes her silky hair out of her eyes and sucks the front of her teeth, in the tapping of her foot and the quick smooths over her clothes.

"Caleb said you'd left them when I called," she explains. "You don't have to walk me through the timeline."

"Caleb said—wait, what? When you *called*?" Jealousy more bitter and distinct than body envy scratches at the inside of my chest. "Do you call Caleb a lot?"

Mackenna rolls her eyes. "It's not like that, princess. I saw your article in the paper. I was already meaning to call after the storm—to check in and all that. See if my favorite tree was still there by the creek. *Anyway*," she says loudly, as if bored by her own story, "after I saw the picture of you three, I really wanted to call and tell them, well, you know." She stares at me as if the end of her explanation is obvious.

I feel silly. Abashed. Significantly less pretty and interesting than she is.

And still wildly jealous. "I actually don't know," I say. "Sorry."

"You *know*, all that mushy, happy-for-you ex stuff." She's gesturing again, as if acting out a one-woman play. "When I broke up with them, I did genuinely want them to be happy. I just knew I was never going to be the woman to do it, and I definitely knew it when I met my two fiancés here in the city a year later. But even though I'm not in love with Caleb and Ben anymore, I still care about them, and I still want them to find a happy ending." She pauses. "Not in the splooging sense,

I mean. Like in the emotional sense. But I guess also in the splooging sense."

I have no idea what to say to this, so I don't say anything at all.

"*Anyway*," she says, again in that bored, impatient-with-herself voice, "I called to say 'I saw your new girl in the paper, I'm glad you're happy, yadda yadda,' and then instead of telling me how happy he is and how Robot Ben has become a human again because of you, he proceeds to wail about how you left them without a fucking word, and now you refuse to talk to them."

My brain snags on a word. "Caleb *wailed*?"

Hand wave. "Sniffled, wailed, whatever. Caleb doesn't *cry*, Ireland. Sniffles from him might as well be sackcloth and ashes."

Ugh. The thought of happy, dimpled Caleb sniffling is enough to tear at my heart. I try not to think about it.

I made the right decision. That's all there is to it.

Mackenna leans forward. "So I have to ask...*why*?"

"Why what?"

"Why, when you three had been happy for a month, did you just pack up and leave?"

I look at her, gorgeous and confident in her body, and immediately feel stupid. "Why do you care?" I deflect.

"Because I feel protective of them," she answers bluntly. "Because I know under those big muscley chests beat two adorable hearts that want to spend the rest of their lives worshipping the woman they love. Because I saw how happy you looked in that picture, and why would anyone abandon people who could make them smile like that?"

Overwhelmed, I press my face into my hands. It's like every feeling at once—every agonizing, earth-ripping emotion I've been burying over the last four days—is scrabbling to the surface.

"I thought it would be better that way," I say into my palms. "For them."

"But why?"

How can I even begin to explain it? The terror and shame of reading those comments? Of knowing that nothing, *nothing*—not my career, not Ben's, not even the simple fact that we loved each other—was enough to stand against my size in the eyes of the world?

"Because I'm fat," I say bitterly. As bitterly and meanly as I can, pouring every drop of pain and fury and shame into the word that I can. "I'm fat."

"So?"

Mackenna says it blandly. Almost uninterestedly.

I look up from my hands, shocked. Actually shocked.

No one has ever said *so?* about my body before.

Not once.

People have protested when I've said the word—*no, you're not fat! Don't say that about yourself!*—or they've substituted euphemisms that amount to the same thing—*you're not fat, you're curvy! Voluptuous! Plus-sized! There's more to love!*

And sometimes in Brian's or my sister's case, it was an excuse to be cruel, to point out if I just wanted it *more*, if I just tried *harder*, I could be thin like them. It was an excuse to tell me I was unhealthy, that I clearly didn't love myself enough, to hint that my fatness actually meant I was a bad person. A weak or greedy person. A worse person.

But never, ever, *ever* has anyone just said "so?" Like instead of me declaring I was fat, I told her I love baseball or that I've never been to Idaho.

I blink.

"So what?" Mackenna repeats. "You're fat. So am I. By the way, nice to meet you. Now what does having a fat body have to do with dumping Caleb and Ben?"

I feel like some kind of rug has been yanked out from under my feet. "I—" I don't actually have words to follow that. I don't have words at all. The only thing in my mind is a vague protest that she doesn't really get it because she's such a cute kind of fat girl, but maybe I'm wrong about that too. Maybe she gets it just as much as I do, because while I see her as having this magically-easier-than-mine body, the rest of the world may not. The rest of the world may see just another body that doesn't fit.

Mackenna squints at me, tilting her head. The light catches again in her glossy, trendy hair, and a new kind of jealousy thrums through me. A softer kind of jealousy than being worried about her relationship with Caleb and Ben. I'm envious of her confidence. Of her utter and complete okayness with who she is. It makes her so fucking cool, so fucking magnetic.

She comes to a conclusion, apparently, bestowing a giant grin on me. "It's that word, isn't it? Fat?"

"Well, I don't—"

"Do you think fat means *bad*?"

206

"I mean, I—"

Hand wave. "It's just a word, princess. A word like *tall* or *short* or *Nebraskan*. It's an adjective that doesn't have to mean anything negative. The world thinks that fat is the worst thing a woman can be, but the more we use the word like a neutral description, the more we say *fuck you* to that idea."

"But," I say, "it's one thing to say it about yourself, you know, to use it as a hashtag and make it your choice. But other people don't use it like that."

"Aha," Mackenna says triumphantly and stabs a finger up into the air. "I knew it was about that article!"

I flush.

"Let me guess... You read the comments?"

"Yes," I mumble. "I know. It was stupid to."

She gives me a rueful kind of smile. "It's okay to forget to expect the worst sometimes."

I let out a long breath, staring past her and out the window. "I felt so idiotic after I did. Because I've spent this year trying to be someone more like you. Confident and happy in my body, like all the body-positive people I see online. And I thought I'd done it! I thought I was over ever feeling bad about my body again—but all it took was one freaking picture."

"And a hell of a comments section," Mackenna adds.

Sigh. "And that."

"Look, princess, body positivity doesn't mean you flip a switch and walk around feeling great for the rest of your life. It's not even really about feelings at all. Body positivity is about what you *do*. It's about daring to live your life as you are—not fifty pounds from now, not six dress sizes from now. And there are going to be days when every bad feeling comes back for you again. When you feel all the messy, hopeless things you thought you were past feeling. Those are the days you *do it anyway.*"

"Do what?" I ask, my voice bleak. "What is there to do?"

Mackenna practically erupts. "Everything! There is everything to do! You post pictures of yourself, or you dress the way you want, or you push back against a flight attendant who's treating you like trash. You unapologetically pursue your photography career, and you date the people you love, even if other people don't like it. Not because it makes you feel good but because it helps change the world. Do you see? Even just living your life is a radical act. *That* is body positivity. *That* is what matters, not an emotion that can change at the drop of a hat."

I understand what she's saying, although I don't know if I like it. It feels *hard.* It feels unfair.

It feels unfair because it is unfair, I remind myself. *It shouldn't be this way.*

It should change.

Maybe I can be someone who changes it. Who fights against the unfair parts, because what's the other option? To live like I did before? To be and die alone?

I press my fingertips against my eyelids, careful not to mess up my makeup but also wanting to keep the tears inside. "But what about Caleb and Ben? Those trolls and my ex were coming after the tavern online, and I couldn't—" I break off, really about to cry now. "I couldn't bear the thought of Caleb and Ben paying any price to love me."

"And?" Mackenna says.

She says it so matter-of-factly, as if there's definitely something else I need to say, that I don't even question it.

I answer her, as surprised by the words as she isn't. "And what if this was the first time they noticed I was fat? What if they hadn't really noticed before, but then after they learned how everyone else sees me, they would realize they didn't really love me after all?"

And then I clap a hand over my mouth. Where the hell did that fear come from?

Mackenna nods as if she were expecting this. "Well, you're a dumbass if you think they hadn't already memorized your body from head to toe long before this article. They know what your body looks like, Ireland, and they worship it. I promise. Also, look at me!" She gestures to herself. "Do you think I would have dated them—*lived* with them—for years if they were capable of that kind of behavior?"

Her eyebrows are arched in challenge, her mouth pursed in a knowing smirk. She looks like the kind of woman who wouldn't stand for any hint of dickish behavior.

"No, I guess you wouldn't have," I say. A new thought occurs to me. A new fear. "Do—do they only date girls like us? Like a fetish or something?"

The thought makes me deeply unhappy. What if all the wonderful, sexy, ecstatic moments we shared were because they had an unhealthy fascination with my body—not because we were simply Ireland and Caleb and Ben?

"Okay, A of all, I don't like the way you said the word *fetish*," Mackenna responds, doing this thing where she aims her pointer and middle fingers at me and waggles them. "It's very kink-shamey, in general, and I don't stand for that. B of all, I don't understand this need to pathologize people who find fat folks attractive. You wouldn't be asking me if they only dated brunettes or Catholics, so why do we have to label normal desire as something twisted just because that desire isn't for a thin body? And C of all, no." She drops her fingers. "They don't only date girls like us. I went to college with them, and I can tell you they've dated all kinds of girls—even dated a boy once."

I let out a long breath.

"D of all," she says, "I feel like you're asking all the wrong questions."

I'm chewing over all the things she's said to me, so it's in an absentminded voice that I ask, "What are the right questions, then?"

"Will your boss give you the afternoon off, and how fast can you get back to Holm?"

My chin quivers with the force of unshed tears. *God, if only it were that easy.* "You don't understand. I'll make their lives harder."

Mackenna rolls her eyes again. "You won't. But also, that's not your choice to make. What if you did make their lives harder...and they still choose to be with you anyway? What if Ben would rather have zillions of one-star reviews and have you in his arms? What if Caleb wants you in his life no matter the cost? Give them a chance to choose you, because, spoiler alert: they will."

I press my fingertips back into my eyelids again, but it's too late, the tears are everywhere.

Mackenna's voice softens. "You're thinking right now that you don't deserve it. That you don't deserve to be chosen. And I'm not telling you to believe it or to feel like it." I hear her stand up and walk over to me, putting a sisterly hand on my shoulder.

"I'm only telling you to act like it," she says. "Fake it 'til you make it, gorgeous. Act like you deserve to be loved, and I promise, everything else will work itself out."

And then she leaves.

I try to hiccup a goodbye or a thank-you, but I know it only comes out as incomprehensible syllables. All my choices are flickering through my mind like the world's most depressing movie, fueling more and more tears.

Leaving the farm.

Dating a man who made me feel awful about myself. Letting my sister make me feel the same.

And possibly the most life-altering choice I made before I met Caleb and Ben: turning down the photography scholarship.

I've lied to so many people about why—I've said it was because I wanted to stay close to home, because I wanted a marketable major—but the real reason is because I went to visit the campus that spring, and everywhere on the grounds and in the halls were girls who *looked* like artists. They were slender and bohemian. They had long, coltish legs coming out of adorable, spaghetti-strapped rompers and hipbones that jutted above distressed jeans. I was the only fat girl in sight, and suddenly everything about me felt fraudulent. I didn't look like I belonged there, and what if that meant I actually didn't?

I wouldn't have fit in—and I felt that on a literal level as well as a social level—and so I tearfully turned down the scholarship and hid myself someplace safe. Someplace invisible. Someplace where I hoped my body wouldn't matter.

I robbed myself of my own future because I was terrified of what people would think of me in the present.

It's only now, after talking to Mackenna, that I realize I'm about to do the same thing. I'm giving up everything I ever wanted from love because I'm scared. Because I think I don't deserve it.

But you don't have to believe you deserve it. You only have to act like it.

I know I'll have to try to find Mackenna online somewhere to give her a proper thank-you. Because her words...her words have freed me from somewhere I didn't even know I was trapped. They've electrified someplace deep inside, and what I feel burning at my fingertips now is not a *feeling* or even a *belief.* It's something much, much more powerful.

It's a decision.

I push away from the table with tears still wetting my face and go find Drew.

"I need to take the afternoon off," I say, swiping at my eyes and in general trying to look like a professional person. "And maybe the day after that too."

"Of course," he says, his ginger eyebrows drawing together. "Is everything okay?"

"Not yet," I say honestly. "But I think it might be."

Sympathy floods his face. "Do you want me to help? I can call Caleb—"

"No." I'm shaking my head. "Thank you, but I think I need to do this myself."

He nods. "Okay. Take all the time you need—you've got plenty stored up."

I give him a teary smile and then go back to my desk to grab my purse and my keys. I'm practically vibrating with all the new parts of me Mackenna has helped unlock, thrumming with the near-violent need to find my men and tell them— what? That I believed the worst of them? The worst of myself?

Yes. I need to be honest about why I left. But I'll also tell them so much more.

I'll tell them how desperately I love them and how my days at the farm were pure magic and my nights in their bed were pure heaven. I'll tell them I don't want any future without them, and if they're willing to jump into this with me, then I'll jump in too. Feet first, eyes wide open, just like I should have done at the pond.

So long as I'm with them, I'll jump anywhere.

I'm practically running down the stairs of the building to get to my car, wondering if I should call first or just show up at the farm, and it's when I get to the first-floor doors that I hear a sound so achingly familiar that the tears nearly start up again.

The happy, chipper yap of a dog followed by the *rattle-bang* of an old truck.

I push open the door to see Caleb's truck wedged awkwardly between two electric cars plugged into charging ports, Greta-dog sticking her head out the window and barking wildly at the silver streetcar gliding by. Caleb and Ben climb out of the truck, looking like Kansas versions of Adonis, with their broad shoulders and narrow hips, and when they catch sight of me frozen in the doorway, they freeze too. They both have big bouquets of buttery yellow sunflowers in their hands.

None of us move for a long minute—a minute when I quietly panic that I've ruined everything and I've ruined it so thoroughly that they've driven two hours just to tell me they never want to see me again.

Hi, is what I should say.

Sorry, is what I should say.

"I love you," is what comes out. So softly that I'm not even sure they hear it.

And then they're loping toward me with big, half-jogging strides, and I'm suddenly crushed into two sets of strong arms and pressed between two hard, warm chests, the sunflowers crushing in there with me. My chin is taken between Ben's firm fingers, and my face is turned toward Caleb. I'm kissed— passionately, tenderly—with a scratch of soft beard, until my knees weaken and I can barely stand. When I start whimpering against Caleb's lips, Ben turns my face back to his and rewards me with a long, thorough kiss of his own.

"Fuck, I missed you," Caleb groans into my ear, hugging me tighter as Ben continues to conquer my mouth with his. "Missed you so damn much."

We break apart with a gasp, and I'm shocked to see Ben's eyes are just as red-rimmed as mine probably are. I reach up and touch the corner of his eye, where even now a tear is beading. The touch of it is scalding—burning me with regret.

"I'm so sorry," I whisper to them both. "I'm so, so sorry."

"No, *we're* sorry," Caleb says, pressing his face into my neck. "We started this whole mess. We should have never told that reporter we were dating if you didn't want us to. If you don't want to be openly dating two men at once, we get it. We'll have you however you want."

"That's not—" I take a breath and pull back enough so I can see both their faces. "That's not why I left. I'm ready for the world to know I love two men. I was a little surprised by it coming up during the interview, but when I chose to pose for that photo, I chose to be ready. I'm proud to be with you."

I receive two dazzling grins in response to that.

"No, it was more like...I was worried you wouldn't be proud to be with me. That even if you were, it would mean subjecting yourself to all kinds of things..." I trail off because Ben's expression has grown stormy and Caleb's thick eyebrows have pulled together in confusion. "The comments people were leaving on that article, the things my ex said...and Ben, your Yelp page..."

"What's Yelp?" Ben asks, his storminess giving way temporarily to puzzlement. "Is that on Twitter?"

"It's a thing on the internet for reviewing restaurants and stuff? Super popular?"

He shrugs, his face getting dark and thunderous again. "I don't care what happens on a Yelp. Do you think the people in Holm are having drinks at the tavern because of reviews on an internet site?"

Having grown to know the people of Holm over the last month, I have to admit it's unlikely. I shake my head.

"Even if loving you meant selling everything I own and going to work at the meat-packing plant in Emporia, I'd do it. I don't give a shit about what people say or do, as long as I have you. As long as *we* have you."

Caleb's nodding in agreement, pressing his face to the back of my hand, as if he can't bear not to touch me for even a moment.

"Ireland," Ben continues, his voice growing raspier, more pained. "It kills me that you'd ever think we wouldn't be anything other than ecstatic to be with you. I don't know what it's like to be fat"—he uses the word in the same mild, casual tone Mackenna did—"and I can't pretend to know all the ways society makes your life harder because of it, and that means I'll be learning as we go sometimes. But I do know how I feel. I don't love you in *spite* of your body. I love you with it, as you are, and I'll never be anything but fucking proud to be yours."

Caleb assents to this last with a nuzzle of his face against my hand and a murmured, "Me too."

My heart lifts. I knew Mackenna was right about everything, of course, but having it confirmed nearly makes me break into tears again.

"You mean all that?" I whisper to them.

They nod solemnly at me.

"We mean it, peach," Caleb says. "And we'll beat the hell out of anyone who says different."

"And we possibly have," Ben says.

I look up at their faces, mischievous and possessive all at once. "Oh, you didn't."

"We just paid your ex a little visit is all," Ben answers mildly. "He won't be bothering us again anytime soon. And he says he's sorry, by the way."

"I feel like I should scold you," I tell them, shaking my head, "but I have to admit, I'm not sorry."

"Good!" Caleb grins. "Neither are we."

Greta barks and prances around our feet, as if trying to signal that she's also not sorry.

I take in the happy dog and these two perfect, amazing men, who are currently trying to kiss me around their hug-crumpled sunflowers.

"Let's go home," I say, kissing them back. "Let's go home together."

And we do.

EPILOGUE

CALEB

Christmas Eve

"Greta! No! Bad Greta!"

My dog has grabbed the end of Ireland's long scarf with her teeth and is trying to tug it free of its owner, growling a little at the red fabric when it doesn't do as the dog likes.

Laughing, I come over and pry Greta's teeth off the scarf and then banish her to the kitchen to her bed by the wood-burner. Normally we don't get much snow in December here, but as an early Christmas surprise, the skies darkened and rumbled and dumped a good eighteen inches onto our hilly stretch of the plains. Enough snow to cover the long grass on the hills that crest around the farm—more than enough to sled on.

And sled we did, Greta-dog bounding through the drifts around us as we took turns on my childhood Flexible Flyer, and we went down the hill so fast that even Ben giggled.

Ben. *Giggled.*

And now we're back home, red-faced and snow-crusted, and I know exactly what I want to do with the rest of my Christmas Eve. I unwind the rest of the scarf from Ireland's neck as she pulls off her hat. Clouds of silky dark hair glisten with specks of powdery snow, and as she tosses her hat onto the table, I can see several big snowflakes still caught in her eyelashes.

Beautiful.

Ben catches on to what I want to do right away and joins me in undressing our woman. He tugs off her gloves, slowly, finger by finger, and then kisses her red, cold-nipped fingertips until she's shivering from something other than cold. We unzip her jeans and peel the denim from her legs, and I drop to my knees and press my face against the cold skin of her thighs while Ben takes off her sweater.

"Your beard tickles," she says, but her laughter changes into a soft gasp when I mouth the soft triangle between her legs, letting my warm breath blow over the silk that cups her pussy. Even after all these months, she still gets this hitched, surprised breath when I touch her there. It goes to a man's head, all that wonder. And the look on her face when I make her come? Makes me feel about eight feet tall.

I want to see that look now, even though we aren't anywhere near a bed, and I press my lips harder against her and kiss her through the fabric, licking and licking until she's soaked through and rocking her pussy against me.

"Put your hands in his hair," Ben grates out. "He likes that. He likes being your toy, don't you, Caleb?"

My nod has the added bonus of stroking my tongue against her clit, and she cries out, her hand threading through my hair and holding me fast to her cunt.

I obey the unspoken command, sucking her pouting little

bud until her thighs are quivering against my face, and then I hook a finger around the wet fabric and allow myself a taste straight from the source. I slick my tongue between her folds as I coax one of her legs over my shoulder, and she leans back against Ben for balance as I fuck her cunt with my mouth.

"That's it," Ben coaxes darkly. "Open up your pussy for Caleb. Let him inside."

She slides her leg farther across my shoulder, and the plump outer petals of her sex unfurl even more, allowing me to lick deep, right at the very heart of her. I fumble with my fly as I taste her, unable to stop myself from pulling out my erection and giving it a few rough strokes.

Fuck, she tastes good. Sweet, with the tiniest hint of sour and salt. Her pussy is so tight, even around my tongue, and it makes me shudder with anticipation to think of how it's going to feel on my cock. Wet and hot and squeezing me, like her body is demanding my come.

I'll give it to her. Now that we've all been tested and she's on birth control, we can finally fuck raw, and the feeling is like nothing else in this world. My cock gives a hard flex just knowing what it's about to get.

Ireland writhes against my mouth, and I realize Ben has his cock freed too so her silk-covered ass can rub against him. He's got his big hand wrapped around her throat now, and whatever he's murmuring in her ear has her getting more and more worked up. I can taste her need, and I can feel it in the fierce tug of her fingers through my hair.

"Enough," Ben finally growls. "Up to bed. I need to fuck."

Stumbling upstairs, Ben and me shedding clothes as we

go, we kiss and grope and grab until we're all in our bed. I drag Ireland against me so her tits are crushed into my chest, and I lick at the seam of her mouth until she parts it and lets me in. I can never get enough of kissing her, of feeling her lips so soft and yielding against mine, and her tongue like hot silk with her perpetual cinnamon taste from her favorite gum.

I reach down to mold my hand over her cunt, and my fingers brush against Ben's fingers as he plays with the little star of her ass, probing it open a little more roughly and urgently than normal.

He knows what we're going to do tonight, and it's got him all worked up. I can't blame him. I could almost come against Ireland's soft belly right now just thinking about it. But I hold it together long enough for Ben to order Ireland to take my cock and feed it inside her.

There's a moment—always that first moment—when the plump head won't fit. When my erection is too big and her pussy is too small, and the pressure is so insane that I think I might erupt right then and there, before the entire tip is even inside.

I live for that moment.

Holding my cock in both hands, she stirs the swollen head against her opening before she tries again, rocking and circling until finally, finally, I start to sink into her tiny channel.

The hot squeeze of her is like the grip of heaven itself, and I push in, needing to fuck, needing to thrust. With a sucked-in breath, her hands fly to my shoulders, and she holds on as I work the edge off my need by giving her a few rough strokes.

"Hold still," Ben says in a voice that demands obedience.

"She's gonna take me too."

Ireland moans her assent, arching as much as she can while pierced with my length so she can make her little entrance more available to Ben.

The usually stoic Ben isn't immune to the sight. A muscle in his tight jaw jumps as he looks down at us, her intimate place speared by my flesh and her ass presented to him the way he likes. With a harsh swallow, he grabs the lube and slicks himself up until his cock is a glistening column of need, and then he swirls some against Ireland's tight hole for good measure.

"Ready, sweetheart?" he rasps.

"Please," she breathes. "Yes, please."

It's slow work. Each inch makes her squirm and pant, her fingertips digging into my shoulders so deeply that I know I'll bruise, but I'll happily wear the bruises as badges of honor. Every single one is worth the look on her face now, with her eyes hooded and her lips parted and a flush that dusts the apples of her cheeks and the top of her chest.

Each inch is also work for me, because the extra pressure is almost too much for me to handle without coming—especially coupled as it is with the erotic squirm of Ireland on our cocks and the rough, reassuring rasp of Ben's legs against my own. The firm brush of his sack on mine.

Soon, he's fully seated, and you'd never guess the three of us have ever been cold, because now everything is heat and sweat and damp. With long, rolling movements, we fuck Ireland in tandem, keeping her filled and stretched, rubbing each other through the thin, shared wall of her body in a touch more intimate than almost anything else in this world.

It doesn't take long. It never does like this. Ireland says it's like being split in half, but being split in half by an electric rainbow made of orgasms. I don't know about all that, but I do know having her sweet body pressed against me, her clit grinding on its favorite place above my cock, and Ben's erection fucking against my own is more than any man can handle. The moment Ireland comes apart in our arms, we follow, grunting with a few final fast strokes and then erupting inside her. My balls draw up tight as my shaft swells, and then I release wave after hot wave of my seed inside her, spending so hard that my vision grays out around the edges. I let out a satisfied roar as all the sizzling, aching pressure finally relieves itself, and Ben gives his usual bitten-off grunt—the most he ever loses control in bed. I savor the feeling of his cock throbbing so close to mine as much as I savor the lingering flutters of Ireland's pleasure, and I allow both to pull the very last drops of my climax out of my cock.

"God, you're such a beauty," I say, kissing Ireland everywhere, petting her and praising her for taking both of us like such a good girl. Ben echoes my praises, kissing her neck and stroking her hair until she's practically purring. We both slip free from her body in a wet rush, and Ben goes to get things to clean us up.

He and I exchange a look as we do.

It's time.

"What do you say we change into our pajamas and go have some warm apple cider by the tree?" I ask casually. Too casually maybe, because Ben rolls his eyes behind Ireland's back at my bad acting as he scoots back on the bed with a towel.

However, Christmas and everything Christmasy is Ireland's favorite thing, so she just nods happily. "Sounds amazing." And then she rolls over like a princess to let Ben attend to her while I clean off, get dressed, and go downstairs to get everything ready.

A few minutes later, we're around the tree with the fire going and steaming mugs of spiked cider for us all. Greta-dog nestles on the couch next to Ireland, who's cute as a fucking button in her flannel pajamas covered in snowmen, but Ben and I remain standing.

"I can make room," she says, preparing to move. "Or we can put Greta on the floor?"

Greta gives a huff, as if she knows she's about to be evicted.

"Don't move," Ben says in his soldier voice, and Ireland goes still, looking confused. We go over to the tree to get the two little boxes we've nestled in the branches. She blinks at them and then blinks at us.

They're not wrapped, tied only with small red bows, and her breathing speeds up as we pull off the ribbons together and open the boxes together.

As we kneel together.

"Ireland," I say, my mouth suddenly dry with nerves. "I know it's only been five months, and I know it's all moved fast. But I've never been surer of anything in my entire life—that I want to spend it with the two of you."

"We want you to be our wife," Ben continues for me. Tears glimmer in Ireland's eyes as he speaks. "We want to marry you and cherish you and spend forever with you. And I know there will be so much to figure out legally, and I know it will never be the easy road, but it's the only road I want. Marry us, baby. Please."

"Oh," she says, starting to cry in earnest now and putting the back of her hand to her mouth. "Oh God. Yes. Yes, of course."

My sternum cracks open and pure sunshine beams out. I'd hoped she'd say yes, of course—I wouldn't have asked if I thought it was unwelcome, but still—to hear your woman say yes to forever is still the best kind of feeling. My own eyes are wet as Ben and I slide our rings onto her finger, each ring one half of a diamond-studded Celtic knot so that when they're put on together, they make one whole design.

Ireland flexes her hand, enraptured by the glitter of our rings, and it's both unbearably arousing and unbelievably— almost spiritually—gratifying to witness.

Ben is ready to fuck her again, I can tell, but we're not quite finished. I reach into the pocket of my pajama pants and pull out another ring.

It's made of beaten metal that's been hammered and burnished to a dull gleam, as quiet and strong as the man it's going to belong to. I take Ben's hand, which is suddenly shaking, and I slide it onto his finger.

"I love you," I tell him, my best friend and lover and weary, mysterious soldier. "I want all three of us to be married, together, in a ceremony apart from anything we do legally. Maybe only two of us can be married on paper, but in our hearts, it will be all three. Tell me yes, Ben. Tell me yes."

The corner of Ben's mouth hooks up in a smile at my command. "I thought I was the one who gave the orders around here."

I kiss him. Hard. And then Ireland is joining in, and the three of us are kissing with more fierce possession than we ever have before, the firelight catching the new rings and sending beams of reflected light around the room.

"Well, then," I finally manage. "I'm ordering you to order us around for the rest of our lives."

"Yes," Ben says. "Yes, of course, and fuck you, I'm crying now."

He is.

Ireland kisses the tears off his cheeks, and somehow that turns into the three of us on the floor, kissing and grinding and eventually fucking while the fire crackles and more snow spits outside. I catch Ireland and Ben looking at their rings more than once as we make love, and if I felt eight feet tall before, there's no telling how I feel now.

Like the luckiest man alive, the luckiest man who's ever had the privilege of being alive. With my farm and my Clementine-cow and my Greta-dog and my truck.

With my broody ex-soldier.

With my curvy girl.

Lucky doesn't even begin to cover it.

EXCERPT FROM
MISADVENTURES WITH A BOOK BOYFRIEND

I was Oliver Connely, for Christ's sake! A household name—especially if the house had women living in it. For the past decade, my face had been plastered on billboards and buildings around the world and every magazine cover from *GQ* to *Esquire*. I'd walked for top designers in Milan, Paris, and New York. I was at the top of my modeling game.

But today?

Today I could barely pay my rent.

I'd heard of the proverbial "wall" from others in the industry but smugly laughed it off, never believing it would happen to me. After all, I was the most sought-after model of my generation. But my twenty-seventh birthday loomed like a dark cloud on the horizon, and the blustery wind that blew in before the storm took all the modeling jobs out to sea with it.

And now I was the guy scraping together change to pay his fucking cell phone bill.

Well, my agent, Harrison Firestein, might not be calling, but my favorite lounge chair at the pool in my condo complex certainly was. I'd been setting up shop there a few times a week to perfect my tan, relax, and forget about the stress in my life.

Since I actually *was* expecting a call from Harrison, I made sure my phone was charged and then grabbed my backpack and strolled across the complex to the pool.

I usually had most of the place to myself during the week. Everyone in Southern California was so health conscious and worried about wrinkles that sun worshipping had fallen prey to self-tanners and fake 'n bake salons. But I'd grown up in rural Iowa, where the summer was barely a quarter of the year and not a decent four-fifths. I hadn't yet given up appreciation for how the sun warmed my skin and gave me a sense of peace like nothing else in my regular routine.

I usually worked out five days a week, but I took an extra day off this week because—*honestly?*—I just wasn't that into it. It was so much easier for me to get motivated when I knew I had a shoot coming up or a show to walk. Since my phone had been unusually silent, I lacked the drive to hit the weights. Where were the job offers from Harrison?

The pool was particularly busy, and I questioned if I'd mistaken today for a weekday when it was actually a weekend.

No. Definitely not.

Skye Delaney, my best friend and amazing roommate, had been out the door at five thirty this morning like she was every workday without fail. Her punctuality used to annoy me, but I'd learned to admire her for her dedication to her career. I might not like the asshole she worked for, but she loved what she did and made a great wage doing it.

We'd been best friends since sophomore year at UCLA,

and she'd been my rock when my family abandoned me for dropping out—and also through the crazy ride of my modeling career. It probably looked like we should've just hooked up and called it done. Been there. Tried that. We had less sexual chemistry than the leads in a bad rom-com. We could laugh about it now, but at the time, it was a disaster.

As I surveyed the crowd at the pool, a vacant lounge chair near the deep end called to me from across the deck. Three little shithead kids were screaming "Polo" in the shallow end while one of their pals turned in haphazard circles randomly shouting "Marco" to coax out their clap backs. Who was the sadistic bastard that came up with that game in the first place? I sent up a mental *thank you* to the ingenious creator of the AirPods in my backpack that were about to drown out the racket.

A cluster of empty chairs just a few feet from mine could pose a potential problem if those kids took a break and decided to camp out there, but a quick scan of the rest of the pool-goers yielded a view of their mothers across the deck. Two were absentmindedly watching the game in the water; the other two were huddled together, obviously talking about something they didn't want the others to hear.

I loved people watching. I'd done a good amount of traveling in the last few years, and often times I was alone. Making up people's backstories had become one of my favorite pastimes. I didn't even try to get it right. I just tried to make it interesting.

My own parents were two of the most boring adults I'd ever met. They met in high school and had been stuck with each other ever since. When I'd come along as an unwelcome party favor from their senior prom night, any hope of leaving that small town and making something of their lives went down the toilet with the first flush of morning sickness.

If the rest of middle-class America were in the same boat, I'd have begged that sucker to pull a Titanic. In the stories I created, people were happy, had adventures, and made the most out of every day.

A nasally voice broke through I Prevail's rendition of "Blank Space" being belted into my ear canal. "Anyone sitting here?" Judging by the "annoyed mom" look on the woman's face when I opened my eyes, she had already asked more than once. I pulled the little white pod from my ear and gave my practiced grin.

"Oh, excuse me. I didn't realize you had— Hey, what is that?" She pointed at my AirPod.

"They're the new AirPods. Perfect sound without the bothersome cord. They connect to your phone or any other device by Bluetooth."

"Well, I'll be... Janine, check this out!" She looked over her shoulder to her three approaching friends. Apparently, the leader of the posse was named Janine.

The bedazzled word *Diva* on her impossibly white ball cap threw tiny rainbows on her friend's face and chest as she spoke to her. "Honey, don't point at him like he's a piece of meat. I'm sure he has a name. And I saw him the minute we walked in. You'd have to be unconscious not to." Janine gave me a conspiratorial wink, like we were sharing a joke at her friend's expense. Except, when I thought about it further, it was really at mine.

She pushed her way past her friend and offered her hand. "Forgive my friend here. She doesn't get out much. We signed her out for a few hours before the nurses came by with her medication."

I took the offered hand and turned it over to place a light kiss on the slope of her inner wrist, but not before noticing the enormous pear-shaped diamond on her ring finger. And I'm talking enormous, as in "my husband works like a dog and we never have sex, but he buys me whatever I want" enormous. The way her mouth hung open after I grinned at her reinforced my assessment.

"Pleased to meet you, Janine. Oliver—"

"Connely. Shit! You're Oliver Connely!" She stammered and stared, and I had to admit, the effect never got old. For all the emotional scars they'd dealt me, I was eternally grateful to my parents for the physical attributes they'd bestowed upon me. Gene pool for the win.

"I am." I grinned again, motioning to the ladies to make themselves comfortable in the neighboring lounge chairs. It was becoming clear we were going to be spending the afternoon together.

"You live here? In this complex?" Janine commandeered the seat next to mine.

"I do. I'm sorry, but I think you ladies have me at a disadvantage. You already knew my name, and now you know where I live. How about some introductions?"

This story continues in
Misadventures with a Book Boyfriend!

ACKNOWLEDGMENTS

Firstly, I have to thank my amazing agent, Rebecca Friedman, who co-pilots with boundless energy and kindness.

A resounding *thank you* to my heroic editor, Scott Saunders, who cleans up tenses and straightens out straggly subplots with the patience of a saint—and to the rest of the Waterhouse team: Meredith Wild, Robyn Lee, Jennifer Becker, Yvonne Ellis, Haley Byrd, Kurt Vachon, Jonathan Mac, and Jesse Kench. And my eternal gratitude and awe go to Amber Maxwell for creating a gorgeous-as-heck cover for Ireland and all her curves!

An especially deep and humble thanks are owed to Julie Murphy, who spent long, late hours talking over plot points and characterization with me, as well as helping me catalog Channing Tatum's and Adam Driver's best physical attributes.

To Ashley Lindemann, Serena McDonald, Candi Kane, and Melissa Gaston for their tireless toil and love! To the Snatches and other authors who make working in this bananas industry possible—especially Tess and Natalie, who keep plenty of beer and sparkling water in their house for me, and any author who has tolerated my lust for dance

parties on a retreat: thank you. I owe the Kiawah crew a special shout-out for plot help and, in particular, Ally C for helping me with the nitty-gritty details of Kansas farming.

Loving and margarita-soaked thanks to the Jarrett girls—Aunt Paula, Aunt Jan, and my own Grandma Sandra—the farm girls in my own family!

And finally, I have to thank you, the reader. Thank you for going on this journey with me and Ireland!

MORE MISADVENTURES

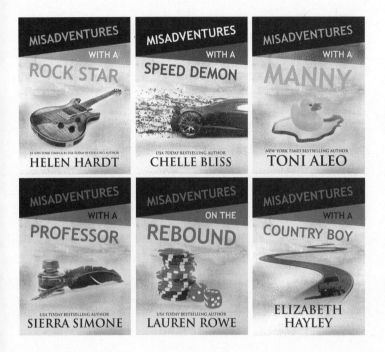